SOME UNCOLLECTED
CASES OF

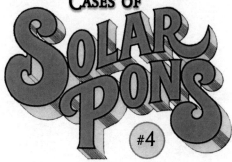

#4

SOME UNCOLLECTED CASES OF

SOLAR PONS

#4

BASED ON THE CHARACTERS AND SERIES
CREATED BY AUGUST DERLETH

BASIL COPPER

EDITED BY STEPHEN JONES

DIP

CONTENTS

EDITOR'S NOTE

Unfortunately, while going through Basil Copper's papers, I was unable to find any of his original manuscripts for the Solar Pons stories. It is possible that these—along with all his correspondence with August Derleth—were amongst the un-catalogued material sent several years ago to the Contemporary Collections repository of the Howard Gotlieb Archival Research Center at Boston University.

We have therefore used the best sources available to us at the present time, including existing texts hand-annotated by the author himself, in the compilation of these volumes. I have also taken the liberty—where required—of returning his work to the English spellings and punctuation that the author originally intended. SJ.

SOME UNCOLLECTED CASES OF SOLAR PONS

THE ADVENTURE OF
THE HAUNTED RECTORY

1

"A BEAUTIFUL DAY, Parker!"

"Indeed, Pons!"

My friend Solar Pons and I were strolling down Regent Street and the sunlight sparkling on the glittering displays in the elegant windows of the shops had prompted my companion's apposite remark. It was indeed a perfect day in early June and as it was my locum's turn to take my rounds and evening surgery I had readily agreed to a morning stroll from our lodgings at 7B Praed Street.

"A never-ending source of fascination; the study of mankind in the raw, Parker."

"Perfectly true, Pons."

"For example, take that gentleman staggering toward us on the opposite pavement. What do you make of him?"

I frowned across the road toward the source of Pons' interest.

"Strange indeed, Pons."

"Is it not, Parker. Let us just have a small display of that ratiocinative power you have been cultivating of late."

"You do me too much honour, Pons."

I frowned again at the man who was dancing about in such an extraordinary manner. He was a little, peppery, red-faced man in formal clothes and with a silk cravat. He carried a stick and from the opening and closing movements of his mouth, he appeared to be muttering imprecations of some sort. He made savage slashing gestures in the air with his stick and his whole manner was so strange and eccentric that the passers-by on his side of the street were giving him a wide berth.

"Some sort of lunatic, Pons?"

"Perhaps, Parker. Let us rather say a man under stress."

"That much is obvious, Pons."

Solar Pons smiled wryly.

"*Touché*, Parker. The pupil will soon be outstripping the master. But just look more closely. Does not the solution rapidly present itself?"

I looked again at the peppery little man dancing about on the opposite pavement. A dark-coated person had appeared at the doorway of a shop on the far side of the way and appeared to be wringing his hands.

"I give up, Pons. I find it quite impossible to find any logical reason for such goings-on."

Solar Pons' eyes twinkled as he stood regarding the small knot of spectators and the little red-faced man.

"It is a fairly common occurrence, Parker. The Duke of Porchester has been having a little altercation with his tailor. There is nothing like sartorial disagreement to provoke anger among certain members of the *haut monde*, my dear fellow. And when I see such an ill-fitting jacket on an otherwise impeccably groomed gentleman, his rage becomes understandable."

I gazed at Pons open-mouthed.

"How on earth can you tell all this from a cursory glance across the street, Pons?"

"By using my eyes, Parker, and drawing the correct conclusion from the data so presented to me. It is not so very difficult but one needs to relate the circumstances to their background. I also have the advantage of knowing something of the relationships involved."

"Relationships, Pons? And how could you know this angry gentleman is the Duke of Porchester?"

"Well, Parker, if you will kindly direct your glance to the adjacent kerb you will see a very palatial vehicle known as an Isotta-Fraschini. The irate gentleman was certainly on his way toward it, for the chauffeur was opening the door for him when the Duke changed his mind."

"How do you know he is the Duke, Pons?"

"For the simple reason that his coat of arms is emblazoned on the door panel. It is extremely distinctive and unmistakable even at this distance. I have made something of a study of such heraldic emblems and the three griffons and the pomegranate are unique in heraldry. My attention was then directed to the gentleman himself and I recognised him from the recent photographs in the newspapers."

"Newspapers, Pons?"

Solar Pons smiled benevolently at the red-faced gentleman, who was now dancing angrily halfway between the car and the dark-coated man in the doorway.

"There has been some controversy in Savile Row, Parker."

"I must confess I am all at sea, Pons. What has Savile Row to do with Regent Street? And what is that tailor's shop doing there, for that matter?"

"Ah, there you have unwittingly hit the crux of the affair, Parker. The Duke is a sharp if eccentric dresser and he had quarrelled with every tailor in Savile Row. The only tailor to suit him was Barker of Barker and Fromset. In the end the Duke persuaded this old and distinguished firm to move their principal premises into Regent Street. From what I gather he has provided the money himself. But it has apparently not taken long for him to fall out with his new partner. Ah, there is Mr. Barker extending the olive branch."

As he spoke the dark-coated man advanced from the doorway of the tailor's establishment, making placatory gestures. The Duke shrugged and the other made some adjustments to his jacket. A few seconds later, the two men disappeared into the shop, the chauffeur slammed the door of the sumptuous motor vehicle and Regent Street resumed its normal placid appearance, the flow of pedestrians going smoothly forward.

"A grotesque little drama, Parker, not without elements of French farce," said Solar Pons reflectively. "And certainly enlivening our walk. A microcosm of the human comedy, one might say."

"There is no getting round you, Pons," I said. "If anyone other than you had sketched such a story for me, I should have been highly sceptical."

"You are at liberty to check the facts, Parker, if you wish. We have only to step over the way, as the Duke is not unknown to me."

I smilingly declined the offer.

"I have no doubt everything you said is correct, Pons. It is only that I occasionally find your infallibility somewhat galling."

Solar Pons gazed at me sombrely from his deep-set eyes and shook his head.

"Hardly infallible, Parker. I have had my share of failure. It is just that I seldom venture an opinion until I am absolutely sure of my ground."

We were both silent until we had reached the lower end of Regent Street and were skirting Piccadilly Circus. Pons glanced at his watch as we turned down into Haymarket.

"Such a promenade is a great stimulator of the appetite, Parker. What do you say to a spot of lunch at Simpson's?"

"The idea is an admirable one, Pons."

"Is it not, Parker. Simpson's it is. Then I really must return to Praed Street as I have a client coming to see me at three o'clock. Are you free this afternoon? If so, I would like you to be present."

"Nothing would give me greater pleasure, Pons. Something interesting?"

"I have high hopes, Parker, high hopes."

And he said nothing further on the matter until we had returned to 7B.

2

It was just a quarter-past three and Pons was showing signs of impatience when Mrs. Johnson, our amiable landlady, announced my companion's visitor. The tall, pale young woman she ushered in bore a marked look of suffering on her features. She would have been extremely attractive otherwise, with her tawny yellow hair that fell over her shoulders, her full lips and white, perfect teeth. As it was, she had a drawn expression about the face and a lurking fear in her hazel eyes, which glanced quickly about her as though half-afraid of what she might see.

"I fancy the young lady could do with some tea, Mrs.

Johnson," said Pons, looking at our visitor sympathetically and ushering her over to a comfortable chair.

"I will see about it at once, Mr. Pons," said our landlady, bustling out.

"It was good of you to see me, Mr. Pons," said the young lady in a low, cultured voice, sitting down and taking off her long white gloves. She was plainly but well dressed in a high-busted suit, fashionably cut, of some light material appropriate to the weather, and appeared more at her ease by the minute.

"From your letter it seemed that your problem was so grave it could brook no delay," said Solar Pons. "Miss Stuart, this is my very good friend and colleague, Dr. Lyndon Parker. Miss Elizabeth Stuart of Grassington, Parker."

I came forward to shake the young lady's hand. We waited a few minutes, Pons talking of trivial matters, obviously to put the girl at ease. When Mrs. Johnson had brought the tea-things and withdrawn, Pons passed a cup to our client and seated himself in his favourite chair. His deep-set eyes never left her face.

"For the benefit of Dr. Parker, Miss Stuart, it might be as well to recapitulate the contents of your letter. I shall need a great many more details before being able to come to any definite conclusions but it would appear a problem which presents unusual points of interest."

Miss Stuart sipped her tea, a frown furrowing the smoothness of the brow.

"It is rather more than that, Mr. Pons," she said.

Solar Pons smiled wryly, tenting his lean fingers before him.

"Pray take no offence, Miss Stuart. I speak purely from the viewpoint of the private consulting detective. It is obvious that you have been through a good deal."

"Indeed, Miss Stuart," I added. "You have our sympathy."

The girl smiled shyly. The shadows seemed to lift from her face.

"I am sure of that, Dr. Parker. Oh, gentlemen, if only you knew how I have suffered these past months."

"Pray tell us about it in your own words," Solar Pons invited.

He leaned back in the chair, the sunlight at the window turning his alert, aquiline features to bronze.

"Well, gentlemen," the girl began hesitantly, "as I indicated in my letter, I live in a small village near Haslemere in Surrey, where my father was Rector!"

"Was, Miss Stuart?"

The girl nodded, the sadness returning to her face.

"Father died suddenly, under tragic circumstances, about two years ago. Fortunately, the house in which we live belonged to my parents and was not part of the living or I do not know what Mother and I would have done. Father had small means and had contributed to a pension fund and we have contrived to manage, with my teaching work."

"I am glad to hear that, Miss Stuart," I commented. "It is very often difficult when the head of the family dies under such circumstances."

"What were the circumstances?" interjected Solar Pons crisply.

The girl looked momentarily startled.

"I do not quite understand, Mr. Pons."

"Of your father's death, Miss Stuart."

"There was a crash one evening, during the winter-time. Mother ran in, Father was in the study, consulting some old books. He was lying near the bookcase, quite dead by the time Mother got to him, a Bible open at his feet. She swore he had been frightened by something, there was such a look of terror on his face."

"I see."

Solar Pons' face was sombre as he stared at the girl.

"What was the medical opinion?"

"Our family doctor said it was a heart attack, Mr. Pons. Such an expression was common in angina cases, he said."

"That is perfectly true," I interposed. "Though I can imagine your mother's distress."

"It was a difficult time, Dr. Parker," the girl said quietly. "But it was not of that I wished to speak. You have my letter there, Mr. Pons?"

"Indeed," said my companion, producing a pale blue envelope from his inside pocket and opening it. "You speak here of terrifying, inexplicable events which have afflicted you and your mother. Pray tell us about them."

"They began back in the winter," the girl continued. "On a dark day of wind and driving rain. Our house, though a pleasant Georgian edifice, is quite near to the churchyard and from some windows, particularly the study, looks out on a sombre view of ancient trees and tombstones with the church beyond."

She paused as though the recollection of something too deep for words had disturbed her. I took the opportunity of rising in the brief interval to pour her another cup of tea. Miss Stuart sipped gratefully for a few moments before resuming.

"I had heard a tapping sound some while before but had thought little of it, because of the noise of the wind. Mother was lying down upstairs before dinner. Hannah, our housekeeper, was in the kitchen. It was a little after dark and I had been reading by the fire in the parlour. I suddenly heard a loud cracking noise. It was somehow connected with the tapping sounds and appeared to come from my father's study.

"I ran in, conscious of wind and flapping curtains. A great shadow seemed to sweep across the room. I put on the electric light and was startled to see that the French window was open and banging in the wind. I secured it and drew the curtains. It was only then that I became aware that some books, tumbled possibly by the wind, were lying on the carpet. I replaced them on the shelves and tidied up."

Solar Pons had sat intent during this recital, his eyes never leaving Miss Stuart's face.

"You saw no one, Miss Stuart?"

The girl shook her head.

"Not on this occasion, Mr. Pons. But from the latter incidents, it now seems evident that someone had slipped the catch of the study window. I thought at the time that it had been left unsecured."

"I see. Pray continue."

"Well, Mr. Pons, I thought little of the incident at the time. Two days passed and again I was reading in the parlour. It had been dark for an hour or so and I had reached the end of my book and decided to seek another from the library in the study. As I neared the door, however, I heard the same tapping as on the previous occasion. I refrained from switching on the light and walked into the room. Then there was a scratching noise from the direction of the window.

"It had a thick curtain over it, Mr. Pons. I walked across and pulled back the curtain. There was just enough light for me to see a hideous hand pressed against the glass. It was something I shall never forget, Mr. Pons. This misshapen hand with a white scar on the thumb, furtively trying to force the window in the night."

There was an awkward silence as our client broke off. Solar Pons leaned forward in his chair, a sympathetic expression on his face.

"As I said, you have obviously been through a great deal, Miss Stuart. Such an experience would have been enough to unnerve anyone. You summoned the police, of course?"

The girl nodded.

"Naturally, Mr. Pons. The cry I made obviously startled the man trying to break into the house because the hand was immediately withdrawn. Our local police sergeant was soon around and he and a constable searched the grounds and churchyard but nothing was found."

"There was no footprint or trace outside the window?"

Miss Stuart shook her head.

"There is a flagged terrace outside the French window, Mr. Pons, which would have retained no imprint. Both my mother and I were upset and shaken by the occurrence and I then remembered the earlier incident. The sergeant felt it might have been a passing vagrant, though he gave me the impression he thought me merely a fanciful woman. When you see the house, Mr. Pons, as I hope you will, you will realise it is rather gloomy."

"Quite so, Miss Stuart. The police discovered nothing, then?"

"The Sergeant had inquiries made but there was no trace of the man with the scarred thumb. More than a month had passed and though I had not forgotten the incident, it had faded a little from my mind when something else happened. It was late January and I was coming back from the village where I had been shopping. I had gained the garden and was about to put the key in the front door when I heard a scream from the direction of my mother's room.

"I rushed upstairs and found my mother in a state of collapse. She had been in her bedroom and had gone to her window, which was uncurtained. There was a great deal of light shining from the kitchen window below which fell across the flagged area of the garden. Standing four-square in the light below her was an evil-looking man with a beard. My mother said he turned his eyes up toward her as she looked out and she had seldom seen such malevolence on a human face. In fact she said it was more like a wild beast than a human being."

Solar Pons tented his fingers in front of him and leaned forward in his chair.

"So this man would have been in the garden at about the same time you were putting your key in the front door?"

"It would seem so, Mr. Pons. I telephoned the police, put on the porch light and rushed out into the garden with one of my father's walking sticks, but could see nothing."

"That was extremely brave but very unwise," said Solar Pons sombrely.

"I realise it now, but I was so indignant on my mother's behalf at the time, Mr. Pons," said our fair visitor. "Another search was made; again it resulted in nothing. I was beginning to have a feeling of persecution by this time. Why should this creature be hanging about our house and what could he hope to achieve by breaking in? We are not rich and there are many more imposing houses in the district. Though my mother and father collected some nice pieces of china and silver, there is little at The Old Rectory to attract a thief and my father was certainly not rich in monetary terms."

"Pray compose yourself, Miss Stuart," said Pons soothingly. "This is what I hope to find out."

"Then you will take the case, Mr. Pons?"

"By all means, Miss Stuart, though I would prefer you to repeat the story to its end in order that Dr. Parker should be fully *au fait* with the circumstances."

"Certainly, Mr. Pons," the fair girl said, a flush on her cheeks, looking quickly at me.

"Nothing else happened until about mid-April. Again, it was dusk. I had been for a walk across the heathland, which has very pretty views. I came up the garden path, but walking in the strip of lawn alongside. It was nearly eight o'clock and a beautiful evening and I suppose I did not want to break the spell by making a noise.

"There was only the sound of a few birds going to their nests and a trace of light still lingered in the sky. I was up near the front door when my spaniel, who had been with me, suddenly barked. At the same moment the door of an old garden shed we have, up near the kitchen entrance, opened, blocking the view along the flagstone walk. Someone went away, walking very quickly in the dusk. By the time I got to the shed there was only a vague shadow going through the gate to the churchyard. The dog rushed off barking excitedly, but returned in a very short while, looking crestfallen."

"Hmm."

Solar Pons sat pulling the lobe of his right ear with his right hand as he frequently did when concentrating.

"You looked in the shed?"

"I did, Mr. Pons. There was nothing of any significance that I could see. An old box had been pulled out, undoubtedly for someone to sit on. It crossed my mind that someone had been keeping observation on the house through a crack in the door, waiting until dark."

"An exceedingly unpleasant business!" I said, unable to contain myself any longer.

"I am inclined to agree with you, my dear Parker," said Solar Pons, frowning at Miss Stuart. "Once again, you displayed commendable courage. Did you inform the police on this occasion?"

Our visitor shook her head.

"I am afraid I did not, Mr. Pons. I have little faith in them by now, and they already regarded me as a fanciful and over-nervous female. It did not seem likely to me that they would be any more successful in tracing the man than on the previous occasions. But I made sure the doors and windows were securely bolted and barred whenever we retired for the night. I did not mention the matter to my mother either, as she had already suffered considerable fright."

Pons consulted the sheet of paper in his hand.

"That brings us to two nights ago, Miss Stuart."

"It has been a heatwave the past two weeks, as you know, Mr. Pons. The day had been sweltering and all the doors and windows into the garden had been left open. Mother took the dog out for a walk and to visit friends on Saturday night. It was Hannah's day off and I was alone in the house.

"I sat in the study reading, curled up in a big wing chair. Dusk came on and the light faded. I stopped my reading but sat on in the chair without the light, it was such a beautiful evening. There was no sound but the faint rustle of the breeze, bringing with it the perfume of flowers from the garden.

"I was still sitting there, half-drowsing in the dusk and the silence, when I heard a faint rustling noise. Something made me behave with caution. I slowly turned in my chair and peeped over the back. I was sitting in shadow and in any case

15

could not have been seen because the chair is a big, high-backed one. Someone was in the room with me, Mr. Pons.

"I shall never forget it to my dying day. The person was standing behind one of the bookcases up toward the French windows, carefully searching through the shelves, because I could hear the furtive sound of books being taken from and replaced upon them. Then, as I looked more closely, half-paralysed with fright, something white caught my eye. The man was evidently reading something, holding the book with his left hand. With his right he supported himself by holding on to the edge of the shelf facing me. Mr. Pons, the patch of white was the same misshapen hand with the scar upon the thumb!"

3

"Great heavens!" I could not help ejaculating. "What did you do?"

"Screamed, of course," said our visitor with commendable frankness. "Screamed with all my might, gentlemen. There was a bang, as though a heap of books had fallen to the floor and a man came scrambling out from behind the shelving, into the light. He was so agitated he collided with the edge of the French doors. He turned his head quickly back over his shoulder. It was a bearded face, all seamed and lined with evil passions, Mr. Pons. The yellow eyes glared hatred and he hissed something back at me as I jumped up from the chair and rushed to the light-switch. Then the creature was gone and there was nothing but the scratching echo of footsteps down the flagged path and the squeak of the garden gate. Of course, I ran out into the sanity of the street but there was nothing there. It was just as though The Old Rectory is haunted, gentlemen."

A long silence was broken at length by Pons.

"It is a remarkable story, Miss Stuart, and it presents a number of features of outstanding interest, as well as a line of reasoning I am inclined to follow. From what you tell me in your letter, you did not call the police on this occasion either?"

Miss Stuart's eyes were sceptical.

"Certainly not, Mr. Pons. I took some advice from a friend in legal practice in the village. I did not, of course, tell him the facts I have just outlined to you. But he immediately advised me to enlist your aid."

"You have done wisely, Miss Stuart."

Pons rose from his seat and paced up and down the room, his empty pipe in his mouth.

"You have no idea what this person could have wanted in your father's study?"

"No idea, Mr. Pons. I cleared up the fallen books before Mother came home. I did not wish to alarm her again. She has gone on a short holiday this week, which was why I suggested a meeting today."

"You examined the books before you replaced them on the shelves?"

"Certainly, Mr. Pons. They were of no importance. Merely old parish records and the like."

"I see."

Solar Pons seated himself again opposite our client.

"What is your reading of this affair, Miss Stuart?"

The young woman, who was obviously now more at ease in our company, put down her empty cup.

"A bibliophile, perhaps, who is out to steal what he can.

There are some quite valuable books belonging to Father, and the French windows are the most obvious access from the churchyard side of the garden."

Solar Pons shook his head.

"I think not, Miss Stuart. A bibliophile, even one with criminal tendencies, would hardly behave in such a manner. There is something far deeper involved here. What say you, Parker?"

"Undoubtedly, Pons," said I. "Though I cannot think what at the present moment."

Solar Pons smiled.

"It is a wise man, Parker, who refrains from committing himself at such an early stage of the game. Are you free to accompany me to Surrey? You have no objections to Dr. Parker accompanying us, Miss Stuart?"

"Good heavens, no, Mr. Pons. I should be delighted. Mother is away, as I have said and Father's old room is always empty. There will be plenty of space for you both, if you do not mind simple cooking."

Solar Pons smiled warmly across at me.

"I can assure you we are not in the least fastidious, Miss Stuart. How are you placed, Parker?"

I rose to my feet.

"My locum owes me a favour or two, Pons. I have no doubt he will be agreeable to taking over for a further day or so."

Solar Pons rubbed his hands together with enthusiasm.

"Excellent! That is settled, then. If you will give us an hour, Miss Stuart, we will be entirely at your service."

"I am most grateful, Mr. Pons. There is a train just before five o'clock, if that will suit."

She hesitated a moment and then went on, almost shyly.

"If only you knew what your coming means to my mother and myself, Mr. Pons. It is almost as though a ghost is hovering over the house."

Pons smiled sympathetically and put his hand on the young lady's arm.

"You must not impute too great a power to me, Miss Stuart. My friend Parker is apt to let his enthusiasm run away with him when chronicling my modest adventures. And we may draw a blank."

The girl shook her head.

"I do not think so, Mr. Pons."

Solar Pons' eyes were fixed unwinkingly upon her.

"You believe this man will come back again, Miss Stuart?"

Our client lowered her eyes.

"I feel certain of it, Mr. Pons."

"And yet earlier you felt a casual intruder might have been involved. That does not sit with my reading of the situation."

Miss Stuart looked temporarily embarrassed.

"I do not really know what to think, Mr. Pons. Sometimes I feel the strain will be too much for me altogether. You see, Mr. Pons, my mother has been far from well since my father's death. I have had to hide my deepest feelings from her. If she really knew what I suspected she would be close to collapse."

Solar Pons nodded.

"Do not distress yourself, Miss Stuart. I understand. You have to pretend to your parent that nothing sinister is involved. Yet you really feel there is a deeper motive behind it all."

The young woman smiled gratefully.

"That is it exactly, Mr. Pons."

Solar Pons rubbed his thin fingers briskly together and looked at me approvingly.

"Well, Parker, I fancy we are a match for any intruder, tramp or no. And just bring along your revolver if you will be so good."

He chuckled as he turned back to our client.

"The sight of Parker's stern features over the muzzle of that weapon is a great pacifier of the baser passions, Miss Stuart."

Within the hour we were on our way to Surrey and Pons sat silent, his sharp, clear-minted features silhouetted against the smiling countryside which flitted past the carriage windows in the golden evening sunshine. We alighted at a small, white-painted country station where a pony and trap was evidently awaiting our arrival and, having stowed our overnight bags, we were soon clattering through the undulating terrain which was permeated with the clean scent of pines.

The tall, taciturn driver did not say a word the whole journey after his grunted greeting to Miss Stuart and we were almost at our destination before our client herself broke silence.

"We are just coming to the village of Grassington, Mr. Pons. We live some way from Haslemere, as you see."

"Indeed, Miss Stuart," said Pons, shovelling blue, aromatic smoke from his pipe back over his shoulder, his eyes focused on the huddle of roofs which lay ahead over the patient back of the glistening roan in the shafts.

"It would be harder to imagine a more delightful spot."

It was, as my companion had indicated, like something out of a picture postcard. A small, timbered High Street, the houses ancient and beamed; a huddle of shops; an ancient square sleeping in the sunshine; contented villagers strolling in the early evening air; and the tower of the ancient Norman church dominating it all. We rattled briskly down the main street, passing a handsome tile-hung inn with its gilded sign of the maypole and turned into a narrow side-street, the horse evidently knowing the way without the driver's signalled instructions on the reins.

The Old Rectory turned out to be a handsome, rambling, tile-hung edifice, of L-shaped construction, set back from the wall of the old graveyard in a large and charming garden but one that was rather shadowed too much by old and massive trees which kept much of the light and air from it.

As we drew up in front of the white-painted gate which bore the name of the house in black curlicue script, I saw that in winter the house would have a melancholy aspect, not only from the trees but from the churchyard, whose lugubrious marble images of angels and cherubs stared mournfully over the low, lichen-encrusted wall.

"Come along, gentlemen!" said Miss Stuart, her spirits quite restored as she led the way up the flagged path while the pony clopped its way round to a stable at the rear of the premises. The white-painted front door was already being opened by a cheerful, middle-aged woman with her hair scraped back in a bun.

"This is Hannah, our housekeeper and very good friend," our client explained. "This is Mr. Solar Pons and Dr. Lyndon Parker, who will be staying with us for a few days."

"Delighted to meet you, gentlemen," said Hannah shyly, extending her hand to Pons and then to me. "I am sure that I will do my best to make you comfortable."

Solar Pons smiled, looking round approvingly at the light and comfortably appointed tiled hall into which we had been ushered.

"You will not find us fastidious, Hannah, I can assure you."

"No, certainly not," I added, aware of Miss Stuart's smiling face turned toward me. She seemed to have recovered her spirits greatly.

"Tell me, Hannah," Solar Pons continued, "Miss Stuart has told me something of the troubles you have been undergoing the past few months. What is your reading of the situation?"

"Well, sir," said the housekeeper hesitantly, glancing at her mistress as though for tacit approval. "It is not really my place to give an opinion, but there is something strange and sinister about it. I know Miss Stuart will forgive me, but why should the same man—and it is the same man by all accounts— return again and again to this house to commit mischief? It isn't natural. And I will swear on the Bible that he is no common burglar."

Pons nodded significantly, glancing from the housekeeper to Miss Stuart.

"Well said, Hannah. That is exactly my opinion and I am glad to have it confirmed by one so obviously sensible and level-headed as yourself. If you can remember anything specific about these events which you feel might assist me, I should be glad of any confidence you might care to make."

"Certainly, sir," said Hannah, taking our cases and retreating up the wide staircase with them. "And I am so glad that you could come."

Pons remained staring after her for a moment. Then Miss Stuart led the way through into a long drawing-room, whose windows, open to the garden with its drowsy hum of bees in the late afternoon, spilled golden stencils of light across the carpet.

"We will take tea immediately, gentlemen, if you wish. And then I presume you would like to examine the study, Mr. Pons."

Solar Pons sat down and tented his thin fingers before him, his eyes raking the room.

"By all means, Miss Stuart. And then I have a fancy to take a stroll about the church before dark."

Our client, who sat by the empty fireplace, which was filled with a great bowl of scarlet roses, smiled. She patted the small, bright-eyed spaniel which had wandered in from the garden.

"Anything you wish, Mr. Pons."

Solar Pons leaned forward as the housekeeper reappeared with a tea-trolley.

"Please do not raise your hopes too high, Miss Stuart. Nothing may happen while we are here. But I will do my best."

"You are being too modest, Pons," I said. "I am sure you will soon have the answer to these baffling events."

"As always, you do me too much honour, Parker."

And he said nothing more until we had finished our tea.

❧ 4

Afterward, Miss Stuart conducted us to a large, handsome room on the ground floor, whose French windows opened on to the flagged terrace of which she had already spoken.

"This is the study, Mr. Pons," she said nervously.

My companion nodded.

"Where all these alarming things happened, Miss Stuart. Well, perhaps now we are on the ground we shall make sense where all has seemed opaque hitherto."

"Let us hope so, Mr. Pons."

Solar Pons looked round keenly, his eyes running over the serried ranks of musty ecclesiastical volumes, many in leather bindings, which ranged across from floor to ceiling. In the corner was the tall leather wing chair in which our client had sat on the fateful evening she had heard the intruder furtively rummaging among the books. But tonight, in this beautiful June weather, the library was a pleasant, placid place, with the mellow sunlight coming in through the open French windows and bringing with it the scent of roses.

Solar Pons had his powerful magnifying lens out now and ranged round the room, watched in silence by Miss Stuart. He moved swiftly down the shelves, his keen eyes darting here and there and then moved out on to the terrace, examining detail quite invisible to me. He straightened up, dusting the knees of his trousers, and came back into the room.

"This is where you say the bearded man stood, Miss Stuart?"

"Exactly, Mr. Pons."

Pons turned to me. He stood about four feet in from the French windows, in front of a long, free-standing bookcase which made a shadowy aisle and divided this portion of the large room in two.

"And whereabouts were the books you spoke of, Miss Stuart?"

"On the third shelf. Here, Mr. Pons."

The fair-haired girl was at our side now and gravely took down a section of books about a foot long.

"As near as I can make out, Mr. Pons, these were the books dropped only two nights ago. It all seems so vivid and horrible and yet it could have been years back."

"Quite so, Miss Stuart," I murmured. "It is often so with a shock to the nervous system."

Pons took the proffered books from Miss Stuart's arms and carried them over to an oval mahogany table, examining them carefully, frowning in concentration the while.

"Hmm. There does not seem much out of the way here, Miss Stuart. *Commentaries on the Epistles; The New Psaltery;* The Holy Bible, King James edition; *Travels in the Holy Land.*"

Miss Stuart shook her head.

"As I said, Mr. Pons. All the rare editions are in this central case down near the fireplace."

She motioned Pons forward as though she would have shown him but my companion held up his hand.

"Nevertheless, Miss Stuart, we will persist here for the moment, if you please. What do you make of it, Parker?"

I went forward to the table and glanced over his shoulder.

"As you say, Pons, it does not look very interesting."

I took up the Bible but moved round the table rather awkwardly, with the result that the book fell, spilling out two or three slips of paper on to the floor. Pons stooped quickly to pick them up.

"Hullo! What have we here?"

Miss Stuart glanced casually at the material Pons held.

"Probably some jottings of my father's. He was always scribbling commentaries and annotations on odd slips of paper. He often worked on his sermons that way."

Pons sat down at the table and smoothed out the pieces of paper, his brow furrowed.

"You might look in the other volumes, Parker."

I did as he suggested but there was nothing else other than two dusty bookmarks. Solar Pons went on sifting through the papers, deep concentration on his face.

"I am inclined to agree with you, Miss Stuart. A printed programme for a Sunday School outing; some notes for a sermon; an account for Bibles supplied by a religious organisation. This looks like something different, though."

He held up a sheet of white notepaper which bore what looked like a set of inked verses with numbers. Pons looked at it in silence, his eyes bright.

"Is this your father's hand, Miss Stuart?"

The girl took the paper, smoothing it out, her face puzzled.

"No, Mr. Pons. This is certainly not Father's hand, though it has a certain familiarity. But I cannot recollect ever seeing it before. Perhaps it came with the Bible. Father often bought second-hand books and they sometimes had strange things in them."

Solar Pons nodded.

"Perhaps you are right. However, I will keep this paper if you have no objection. And in a little while Parker and I will take a stroll over to the church."

"Certainly, Mr. Pons. You will find me in the drawing-room when you return."

And with a quick smile, Miss Stuart quitted the room through the French windows and we were alone. Solar Pons sat, his brows heavy, the slip of paper on the table in front of him.

"Just take a look at this, Parker."

I sat down next to him and stared at the lettering.

"It looks like a set of Bible verses, Pons."

"Does it not, Parker. Corresponding to the text in this Bible, no doubt."

"Nothing unusual about that, surely, Pons."

"Perhaps not. But kindly peruse it if you will have the patience."

I did as he bid but I must confess I was no wiser when I had finished. This is what I read:

And as he went out of the temple, one of his disciples said unto him, Master, see what manner of stones and what buildings are here.

St. Mark, 8.

Therefore I said unto the children of Israel, Ye shall eat the blood of no manner of flesh.

Leviticus, 6.

An ungodly man diggeth up evil; and in his lips there is as a burning fire.

Proverbs, 4, 5.

Yet gleaming grapes shall be left in it, as the shaking of an olive tree, two or three berries in the top of the uppermost bough, four or five in the outmost fruitful branches there of.

Isiah, 18, 22, 29, 32.

All these were of costly stones, according to the measures of hewed stones.

Kings, 13.

The fining pit is for silver, and the furnace for gold; but the Lord trieth the hearts.

Proverbs, 6, 11.

I handed the slip back to Pons.
"I am afraid it means nothing to me, Pons."
Solar Pons smiled, thrusting the paper into his pocket.

"Yet much may be made of it, if one reads the riddle aright, Parker. May I commend to your attention that excellent English novelist, J. Meade Faulkner. His adventure yarn *Moonfleet* is one of the finest in the language, excepting only Stevenson."

"You astonish me, Pons."

"It would not be the first time, Parker. But let us just stroll to the church. It is such a fine evening and we must take advantage of the light."

He led the way through the French windows and after signalling to Miss Stuart, who was standing near the garden gate talking to a tall fair-haired man in the roadway, and indicating our intentions, he hurried down the pathway which led to the church. I followed and we strolled through the slumbering old graveyard, with its grey, tumbled tombstones, along a red-brick causeway to the entrance of the Norman edifice.

The huge iron key was in the lock of the massive, studded door and it sent echoes reverberating from the interior as Pons pushed it back on its hinges. The building was a surprisingly large one and paved with huge flagstones in which memorial slabs were set. The inscriptions were worn away with the feet of the centuries and as I puzzled over one pious Latin obituary, Pons wandered down the central aisle, his progress sending back echoes from the vaulted ceiling.

When I rejoined him he was standing at the entrance of a small side-chapel, pondering over a white marble statuary group. It represented five or six children with long hair which appeared to be streaming in the wind.

"Rather sombre, Pons," I observed.

"Not surprising, Parker," said my companion drily. "This is

an early nineteenth century stonemason's version of the Darnley children, daughters of a large landowner hereabouts, who were unfortunately drowned in a boating accident in 1816."

"I see."

I pondered the melancholy description in black lettering on the marble base while Pons wandered aimlessly about the chapel, stopping here and there to gaze absently at the floor. We had just turned away when there sounded the beat of footsteps from the curtained vestry to one side and a black-bearded face, from which two red-rimmed eyes stared suspiciously into ours, came rapidly toward us.

It surmounted a massive body clad in a black surplice and a silver cross glittered on the chest. The atmosphere was one of veiled hostility though the voice was civil enough.

"Isaac Stokesby, Rector of this parish. Might I ask what you are doing here?"

"Merely imbibing the atmosphere of this wonderful old building," said Solar Pons courteously. "Solar Pons. My friend Dr. Lyndon Parker. We are the guests of Miss Stuart whose house is across the churchyard yonder."

The Rector drew back and a subtle change of expression flitted across his features.

"Forgive me, gentlemen. There have been some strange goings-on in the village these past months and I always keep a careful eye on strangers."

He extended a powerful hand to each of us in turn.

"A very wise precaution, Rector," said Solar Pons warmly. "Miss Stuart has already told us something of the matter. What do you make of it?"

The Rector shrugged, his dark, bearded face impassive.

"A vagabond, no doubt. But I always keep the church locked

after dark. I would be grateful if you would turn the key when you have finished."

"By all means. Come, Parker, we must not keep the Rector from his duties."

As we walked back through the darkling church, I turned to see the tall, bearded figure still staring somewhat suspiciously after us. Solar Pons rubbed his thin hands with satisfaction. He turned the big heavy key of the main door behind us and stood pensively in the mellow evening sunshine.

"Well, Parker?"

"He seems somewhat of a strange character, Pons," I ventured.

"Does he not? And a rather unusual one for such a quiet spot."

"What do you mean, Pons?"

We had resumed our aimless strolling through the churchyard and Pons paused a moment before replying, shading his eyes as he gazed after the fair-haired man who had been talking to our hostess.

"A military man, Parker," he resumed. "One accustomed to giving orders and commanding men."

I stared at my companion in puzzlement.

"How do you make that out, Pons?"

"He had the ribbon of the Military Cross on his surplice, Parker. He obviously served in the late war and the M.C. does not come up with the rations. If I mistake not the Rev Isaac Stokesby has seen some heavy trench fighting."

"A strange vocation for a man of the cloth, Pons. I should have thought he would have been a chaplain."

"Army chaplains tend the wounded and dying under heavy fire, Parker, and there are many heroic deeds recorded in their annals. But he may have decided to become ordained after the end of the war. It is sometimes so."

"In revulsion against man's inhumanity, Pons?"

"Very possibly, my dear fellow. Now I suggest a stroll to the village inn before putting a few more questions to Miss Stuart over supper."

5

The large oak-timbered lounge bar of The Cresswell Arms was full on this warm, summer evening and Pons and I enjoyed our tankards of cold cider, the scent of jasmine coming in heavy and cloying with the breeze through the open windows. The tall, fair-haired man to whom Miss Stuart had earlier been talking was standing at the bar and had nodded agreeably as we came up to give our order.

Now he made his way to the side-table where we sat and introduced himself.

"Major Alan Kemp, gentlemen. I live just across the green there and am a friend and neighbour of Miss Stuart. I understand you are staying at The Old Rectory."

"Indeed, Major Kemp."

Pons rose and introduced me and the Major sat down at Pons' invitation.

"Allow me to refill your glass."

"That is very kind, Mr. Pons. A Scotch and soda if you please."

The Major chatted amiably as we waited for Pons to return from the bar.

"Your first visit to Grassington, Mr. Pons? Your good health, sir."

Major Kemp raised his glass in a polite toast as Pons and I reached for our second tankards of cider.

"Yes," I volunteered. "It seems a pleasant spot."

"It is that," the Major agreed.

With his sandy moustache, faded blue eyes and fresh cheeks he seemed the very epitome of the retired military man. A red setter slouched on the tiled floor at his feet. Kemp wore a suit of well-cut tweeds, his dark blue shirt, open at the throat, adding an informal touch, while his right hand toyed casually with a leather dog leash as we talked.

"You have known Miss Stuart long?" asked Solar Pons, his deep-set eyes raking round the room.

"Several years, Mr. Pons. We are quite good friends. I was so sorry to hear she had been upset."

"A nasty shock for a lady," Pons added. "Are there any tramps hereabouts?"

Kemp shrugged.

"We get our share through occasionally. My theory is that the intruder was most likely to have been a gypsy. There are several encampments in the neighbourhood."

"Indeed."

Solar Pons' eyes were thoughtful as he stared at the Major.

"That is a possibility, of course. You mentioned that to Miss Stuart?"

The Major hesitated. He drained his glass and stood up. To my mind his expression had changed in some subtle way. There was a darker red suffusing his cheeks.

"It does not seem as if I am in the lady's confidence. She has newer friends in whom to place her trust it appears."

He jerked his head stiffly, with an embarrassed expression.

"Good day, gentlemen."

And he strode out of the bar. I gazed after him blandly.

"What odd behaviour, Pons. Do you think he can have anything to do with this bizarre business?"

"Possibly, Parker. He certainly seems piqued that we are staying at The Old Rectory."

"Perhaps he is an admirer of the lady himself, Pons."

My companion stared at me gravely.

"It is just possible, Parker. She is certainly a very attractive young woman."

Our conversation passed on to other matters and dusk had fallen when we walked back to our hostess' house. An excellent cold salad supper had been prepared in the dining room, served by the housekeeper, and during the meal Pons kept up a bantering conversation with Miss Stuart in which all reasons for our being there were avoided. There was a lull as the fruit and coffee were brought in and I chose the interval to remark on our conversation with Kemp.

It was my impression that Miss Stuart coloured a little as she looked from me to Pons.

"Major Kemp? I hope you did not discuss your business here, gentlemen?"

"Certainly not, Miss Stuart," I ventured. "The Major seemed concerned about you. He volunteered that the man you saw may have been a gypsy."

A troubled look passed across the fair girl's face.

"It is possible, Dr. Parker. As the Major said, there are a number of camps."

"Exactly where?" interjected Solar Pons. "Though gypsies are not the problem."

"Two to my knowledge on the edge of Cresswell Woods. Another down at the old quarry, south of the village."

"I see."

Solar Pons nodded, his thin fingers tented before him on the oak table top.

"Tell me, Miss Stuart, are you quite alone in the world? Except for your mother, that is?"

Our hostess bit her lip.

"There is no one to speak of, Mr. Pons. My father's brother Jeremy used to stay here, years ago. Father did not speak much of him. He was the black sheep of the family, I believe."

She smiled.

"In the classical tradition he emigrated to Australia, I understand."

"I see. You would have been a child at the time?"

"Indeed, Mr. Pons. I remember there was a quarrel between them on one occasion, which was unusual, because my father was a very mild man. After that, Uncle Jeremy no longer came here. I have no doubt my mother would know more."

"Pray do not bother, Miss Stuart. It is just that I wish to get a complete picture of your household."

Pons glanced at the cased grandfather clock in the corner of the dining room.

"I have a mind to take a moonlit walk after that excellent supper, Parker. Would it be possible for me have a front door key, Miss Stuart?"

"By all means, Mr. Pons."

Miss Stuart looked a little startled and Pons smiled to reassure her.

"It is not yet nine o'clock. We shall be no more than an hour or two and in any event will be back inside these walls well before midnight."

The girl passed a hand across her face.

"I should appreciate it, Mr. Pons. There are only the two of us here you see and after what has happened . . ."

Her voice faltered and she stopped. Solar Pons rose from the table and put his hand gently on her arm.

"You are in no danger now, Miss Stuart. Just lock all your doors and windows and leave the front door on the latch. I will securely lock and bolt it on our return. Come, Parker."

I followed Pons up to his bedroom somewhat bemused and waited while he rummaged in his suitcase. He produced a small electric torch in a Bakelite case and a flat packet tied in oiled silk.

"I think this will do nicely for our little expedition, Parker. You have your revolver?"

"Certainly, Pons."

"Come along then, my dear fellow."

I followed him downstairs and cut through the garden with increasing puzzlement. We hurried down the path toward the churchyard.

"But where are we going, Pons?"

"To the church, of course, Parker. The key to the whole situation lies there."

"You amaze me, Pons."

Solar Pons chuckled.

"That is only because you have not included Meade Faulkner on your reading list. I will explain later. In case I am wrong."

"You are seldom wrong, Pons."

"More often than you think, my dear fellow."

We hurried up the path between the gravestones in the brilliant moonlight, the homely sounds of the small village of Grassington behind us coming sharp and clear on the warm summer air. There was an agreeable smell of mown grass in the church-yard and the faintest trace of orange-red lingered in the west, as though the sun were reluctant to depart. Gas lamps bloomed in the roadway which skirted the church and we waited as a small group of excited young people—evidently the stragglers from a tennis party—chattered their way along the road.

All was quiet except for the distant drone of a motor car as we came up to the massive porch door.

"How on earth are we to get in, Pons?"

To my astonishment my companion produced a huge iron key from his coat pocket. His eyes were twinkling as he inserted it into the lock.

"I abstracted it earlier, my dear fellow. The Rector asked me to make sure to lock it, you remember."

"We are more likely to be seeing the inside of the village constable's lock-up than the church, Pons," I said a little irritably.

"Tut, Parker, you stand too much upon your dignity. It is a failing I have often observed among the medical profession. Pomposity, like a distended stomach, is all the better for being deflated."

I thought it best not to answer that and a few moments later we were within the darkened church. I waited until Pons had relocked the main door and then crept quietly after him down the central aisle, the pale and cautious disc of his torch-beam dancing across the stone-flagged floors. Pons had a slip of paper in his hand and consulted it quietly as we came to the chapel entrance.

"Let us just work this out, Parker. It should not take long." He handed me the torch and I waited while he again consulted the paper, his lean, eager face alive with interest.

"Ah, yes. It is quite clear. Here are the children. If you would be so good, Parker, as to shine the beam on to the floor here."

I did as he said, considerably puzzled by my companion's strange behaviour. Pons went beyond the Darnley statue, his lips moving noiselessly. He walked along the line of heavy paving stones within the chapel. He gave a small exclamation of satisfaction and bent swiftly to the floor. I joined him, shining the beam of the torch on to a large slab which bore faded carving. One name could be vaguely made out and Pons waited patiently while I deciphered it.

"Why, Pons, this appears to be the entrance to the family vault of the Cresswell family!"

"Does it not, Parker. Ah, yes, it should not be too difficult."

To my astonishment Pons placed the torch on the floor where he could see to work and selected what appeared to be a slim cold chisel from the small pack he had brought from his bedroom. He went round the edges of the slab, frowning the while, until he finally inserted the end of the tool into the faint hairline between the slab and the surround. I put my hand upon his arm.

"Heavens, Pons, you surely do not intend to break into the vault?"

"That is most certainly my intention," Solar Pons replied coolly. "Just stand back, there's a good fellow."

I did as he bade, considerably perturbed, my eyes darting about the dark interior of the church, now silvered with moonlight, while the harsh grating noise as Pons commenced work denoted the pressure he was putting to bear upon the slab.

"There, Parker, if you would be so kind as to add your considerable weight . . . "

I quickly put my hand beneath the edge of the slab, which Pons had levered from the floor, and we swiftly lifted it out on to an adjoining flagstone. It was immensely heavy but did not appear to be bonded in any way, though considerable quantities of dust fell into the gaping hole disclosed. I gingerly directed the beam of the torch downward, exposing a flight of ancient steps. Pons was already through and he reached up to take the torch from me.

I followed him down. The air was dry and musty with a faint aroma as of cloves. We had not gone more than two or three yards before Pons gave a sharp exclamation.

"I do not think we need go into the vault proper, Parker. Unless I am much mistaken this is what we are looking for."

He pointed downwards to where a large bundle wrapped in sacking lay against the wall, on one of the broad stone steps. He approached and lifted one end. There was a chinking noise and he grunted at the weight.

"I think it will take the two of us, Parker."

He pulled aside the sacking and exposed what looked like a large wicker picnic basket. I got my hands under the end and tested the weight. As Pons had indicated, it was considerable. Pons took the torch under his arm and we each lifted one end of the sacking-wrapped hamper. Though it was only a few yards to the vault entrance, I was already perspiring by the time we got there.

Once in the church it was easier, for we could both stretch properly, which we had been unable to do in the confines of the staircase. Only a quarter of an hour had passed before we replaced the slab. Pons was most meticulous about restoring the area to its former state and was not satisfied until we had carefully brushed the dust back into the cracks round the slab.

I was impatient to be off but he was at last satisfied and we carried our heavy burden back through the darkened church to the main door. There was no one about and Pons locked it behind him.

"What will you tell the Rector?" I asked.

"That I inadvertently took the key with me," said my companion.

He smiled.

"It is only a white lie, after all."

We got back through the churchyard without mishap. Miss Stuart's house was in darkness except for two lights in the upper storey of The Old Rectory, which undoubtedly came from her bedroom and that of the housekeeper. Pons led the way through into the study, after ostentatiously locking and bolting the front door.

We put our burden on a large oak table in a corner of the library, pulling the heavy curtains across the windows before switching on the lights. We waited five minutes in case Miss Stuart came downstairs but the silence continued unbroken. When he was satisfied that we were unlikely to be disturbed, Solar Pons sat down at the table and lit his pipe.

Blue clouds of aromatic smoke curled lazily toward the ceiling in the warm air as he gazed at the object on the table almost dreamily. He carefully unwrapped the sacking, revealing the big, dusty old hamper.

"What do you make of it, Parker?"

"I am completely in the dark, Pons."

I sat down at the table opposite Pons and studied my friend's lean, ascetic face carefully.

"Victorian hamper, Parker. Not much used. Probably kept normally in the box-room of a large mansion."

"That's all very well, Pons," I replied. "But what does it

contain? No doubt you already know, judging by your mysterious antics tonight."

Solar Pons smiled, his eyes dancing with mischief.

"Gold and silver undoubtedly. Patience, friend Parker. You will know as much as I do within a few minutes."

The handles of the hamper were secured with thick cord but Pons produced a folding knife from the kit of tools in his oilskin pack and swiftly cut them. He opened the lid. I craned forward to look into the interior but was disappointed at seeing nothing but a plain white cloth.

Pons carefully eased the edges of the cloth outward; they had become stiff with the years. I then realised that it was nothing more than a bed-sheet, though the linen was not of ordinary quality. I gave a gasp as the cloth fell away for the overhead light winked back in a thousand reflections from gold and silver surfaces. The whole of the interior of the hamper was stuffed with silver plate; massive silver candlesticks; gold coins; statuettes and other *objets d'art*.

Tissue paper had been carefully placed between the various items but it looked as though the packing had been hastily disturbed, for the owner had undoubtedly thrown the sheet over the top of the material without first covering it with tissue. Pons carefully lifted out a solid silver statuette of a prancing horse, one of a pair, golden sovereigns cascading to the table as he did so.

"Good heavens, Pons!" I exclaimed. "These things must be worth thousands."

Solar Pons nodded, his eyes narrowed.

"Many thousands, Parker. These snuff boxes in the corner are by Fabergé, unless I miss my guess. Just take a look at this."

I glanced at the base of the silver statuette Pons was holding. Apart from the hallmark, something was incised in the surface. It took a moment or two to make it out.

"It looks like a maypole, Pons."

"Exactly, Parker. The same sign as the inn. And the same title."

"I do not follow, Pons."

"Tut, Parker. Learn to use your ratiocinative processes. These are the armorial bearings of the Cresswells."

"But why would they want to put these things in their family vault, Pons?"

Solar Pons concealed his rising irritation superbly.

"Undoubtedly they did not, Parker. This treasure has been stolen."

🖋 6

There was a long silence between us, broken eventually by the church clock striking eleven. As its echoes died away Solar Pons replaced the statuette in the hamper, together with the gold sovereigns.

"Miss Stuart must know nothing of this for the time being, Parker. At least until we have secured our man."

I stared at Pons in rising irritation.

"I am sure I do not know what you are talking about, Pons."

Solar Pons finished rewrapping the hamper in sacking.

"You shall know a good deal more before you leave this room, my dear fellow. Just hand me down that gazetteer from the shelf behind you."

I gave him the volume and he studied it, his brows knotted in concentration through the wreaths of tobacco smoke.

"Ah, here we are. Cresswell Manor. The seat of the 1st Baron Cresswell. Well, we do not require all that ancient history. Ah, here we are. Last of the line, Sir Roger Cresswell, Grenadier Guards, killed in heavy fighting during the first months of the last war. Unmarried, therefore no issue. The empty house was burned down in a mystery fire in 1915. That is significant, Parker."

"I do not see why, Pons."

"That is because you are not applying your mind properly to the problem. It limits the time factor, do you not see. The mansion did not exist after 1915. Therefore, I have only to look between the turn of the century and the outbreak of war."

"For what, Pons?"

"For the date of the robbery, Parker."

Solar Pons had produced his sheet of paper from his pocket and was studying it intently. I recognised it as that taken from the Bible earlier. Pons passed it over to me. Once again I read the baffling set of verses.

And as he went out of the temple, one of his disciples said unto him, Master, see what manner of stones and what buildings are here.

St. Mark, 8.

Therefore I said unto the children of Israel, Ye shall eat the blood of no manner of flesh.

Leviticus, 6.

An ungodly man diggeth up evil; and in his lips there is as a burning fire.

Proverbs 4, 5.

42

Yet gleaming grapes shall be left in it, as the shaking of an olive tree, two or three berries in the top of the uppermost bough, four or five in the outmost fruitful branches thereof.

Isiah, 18, 22, 29, 32.

All these were of costly stones, according to the measures of hewed stones.

Kings, 13.

The fining pit is for silver, and the furnace for gold; but the Lord trieth the hearts.

Proverbs, 6, 11.

I shook my head.

"This still means nothing to me, Pons."

"Simply because you are not using your God-given faculties, Parker. Kindly reach down that same Bible from the shelf there."

I crossed over to fetch it, Pons opening the heavy volume.

"Just check St. Mark, if you would be so good."

I did as he suggested. I looked up again, conscious of the ironical expression of his eyes.

"Why, Pons, this verse does not match at all."

"Exactly, Parker. Which is why I directed your attention to that excellent novel, *Moonfleet*. There the author uses a similar device to indicate hidden valuables. The thing is the simplest of codes."

I looked at the verses again.

"You mean there is another book with the correct verses?"

Solar Pons shook his head.

43

"No, no. The non-existent verses merely indicate the word-order. Do not underline the verses there, for I have another use for that paper, but indicate them on a separate sheet. What does that give you?"

I jotted down the words with mounting excitement. I now read:

TEMPLE CHILDREN DIGGETH UP THERE TOP FIVE
OUTMOST STONES SILVER GOLD.

"Good, heavens, Pons! I see what you mean. It is a cipher."

"It was obvious, Parker. No Rector would have written such corrupt textual references. Therefore the material in the Bible had not been written by him. I saw at once that 'temple' could refer to the church. When we visited the building earlier today I at once noted the statue of the Darnley children. From there it was child's play. The message referred to the three top paving stones by the statue, and then the five most outmost from that, which brought us to the vault slab of the Cresswell family."

"Excellent, Pons."

"Elementary, my dear Parker. We still have only half the puzzle. It now follows that the gold and silver for which one was invited metaphorically to dig was stolen. It is equally evident that the sinister, bearded man of Miss Stuart's encounters is searching for this booty. But who left the message in the Bible and why; and whether he is connected with the searcher is another matter. I have my own ideas on that but they must just wait until we have firmer data."

I gazed at Pons open-mouthed.

"You knew all that before ever we went to the church today, Pons?"

"It was reasonably self-evident, Parker."

Solar Pons sat drawing on his pipe in the heavy silence which followed. The house was quiet except for the faint creaking of timbers and I was absorbed in my own thoughts. Solar Pons rose at length and looked at the clock.

"A brief nightcap, I think, Parker. Things will be clearer in the morning, when I must devise some method to bring our man to us. In the meantime, if you would be kind enough to help me get these things to my room, the sooner they are under lock and key the better."

We breakfasted early the following morning, the brilliant sunlight streaming in through the open windows. The country air was increasing my appetite and I ate a hearty meal. Pons was silent as we sat drinking our coffee, his deep-set eyes apparently fixed on the tower of the church through the trees. Our hostess sat watching us intently. Eventually she broke the silence.

"You have come to some conclusions, Mr. Pons?"

"I have indeed, Miss Stuart. And I must ask for your full co-operation."

"Anything you say, Mr. Pons."

Solar Pons smiled thinly.

"It may sound a little peculiar to you, Miss Stuart, but it is, I think, the only way to bring the intruder who is haunting this house out into the open. What is the evening paper for this area? One that would certainly be read by the local inhabitants?"

"Apart from the national evening newspapers, Mr. Pons, there is only the *Surrey Observer*. Their nearest office is in Godalming."

"Excellent, Miss Stuart. Perhaps we could hire a car in the village?"

"The local taxi man is reliable, Mr. Pons. As you know he is to be found at the railway station most days."

Our client's eyes were fixed upon my companion's face with great intensity.

"What is your plan, Mr. Pons?"

Solar Pons had taken an envelope from his pocket and was scribbling something on the back of it with great vigour.

"I wish to insert the following advertisement in the *Observer*, Miss Stuart. Would I be in time for this evening's edition?"

"You would if the advertisement is at the office by midday, Mr. Pons. That would be early enough for the edition which is out by six o'clock. We get it locally a little after that, as our newsagent collects it from the train."

"I see. It is a great impertinence, Miss Stuart, but I wish to insert the following announcement. I would be glad of your co-operation."

Miss Stuart glanced at the paper Pons handed her and gave a start of surprise.

"It is extraordinary, Mr. Pons. I am in complete agreement, of course, but I do not know what Mother would say."

Solar Pons chuckled.

"She is away, fortunately, my dear young lady. Let us just get Parker's opinion."

Miss Stuart handed the envelope to me and I read Pons' announcement with increasing bewilderment. It was headed RARE BOOKS and ran: CLERGYMAN'S LIBRARY FOR SALE. RARE, ECCLESIASTICAL AND OTHER BOOKS AT REASONABLE PRICES. VIEW ANY TIME WITHOUT APPOINTMENT. STUART, THE OLD RECTORY, GRASSINGTON, SURREY.

I looked up at my companion.

"Extraordinary, Pons."

"Is it not, Parker. Yet I feel this might be just the item to tempt our friend."

Miss Stuart's eyes were sparkling.

"You think the man who broke in might read this and visit here openly in the guise of a rare book dealer or purchaser?"

"Exactly, Miss Stuart. I must force his hand. He must be desperate by this time and will probably grasp at what he would consider a golden opportunity. We cannot just sit here for the next few weeks hoping he might attempt to break in again."

"Of course not, Mr. Pons. You certainly have my permission."

"Thank you, Miss Stuart. I would like you and your housekeeper to remain here all the time, of course, and Parker will be on hand. You must explain that no list has been prepared and let people browse around the study shelves as they wish. Most will be genuine bibliophiles so you need fear no attempts at pilfering."

"But suppose someone steals that Bible, Pons?" I asked.

"That is exactly what I wish them to do, Parker," said Solar Pons. "And to that purpose I shall replace that slip of paper exactly as you found it just as soon as we have finished breakfast. I must also consult the bound files when we visit the newspaper office. They would have records there, Miss Stuart?"

"Certainly, Mr. Pons. It is a large office."

"Excellent."

Solar Pons glanced at his watch.

"We have much to do this morning, Parker. I would be obliged if you would arrange for a taxi to take us to Godalming. In the meantime I must ring Bancroft at the Foreign Office. And Jamison also."

"What on earth for, Pons?"

Solar Pons smiled enigmatically.

"To put one or two small inquiries afoot, Parker. This ghost of the Rectory, as Miss Stuart calls him, has created a good deal of terror. Now we must close the net around him."

7

It was indeed, as Pons had hinted, a busy morning. We drove swiftly to Godalming where Pons spent an hour closeted at the newspaper office. After placing his advertisement he was shown to a small glassed-in office where the bound files of the journal were kept. I left him there to buy one or two items for my comfort, for I did not know how long we were likely to be at Grassington, and when I returned some time later I found him in fine fettle.

He rubbed his thin hands together in satisfaction, his deep-set eyes blazing with excitement.

"There you are, Parker. I was not far wrong in my assessment."

I followed his pointing forefinger to the news item he indicated in the musty volume of 1912 open before him. It was headed: THIEVES STEAL FORTUNE FROM CRESSWELL MANOR. £100,000 GOLD AND SILVER TAKEN.

I read the article with increasing interest. It went into great detail and itemised the valuables stolen with considerable exactitude. There was no doubt in my mind as I finished the account that the missing articles were those Pons had recovered from the church vault the previous night.

"Ten years ago, Pons. It does not say who was responsible for the theft."

Solar Pons looked at me mockingly.

48

"That was too much to hope for, Parker. I have been through the subsequent issues with great care but apart from items in the police inquiries, there is nothing. But then I did not expect it."

His quizzical eyes were turned fully toward me.

"And there would be little on which to stretch my peculiar talents, Parker."

"Perhaps not, Pons, but it would have been helpful, nevertheless."

Solar Pons laughed shortly, folding his sheaf of notes and putting them in his pocket.

"You were ever practical, Parker. But I have a few ideas up my sleeve. We must not forget the sight which caused Miss Stuart's father to drop dead of shock."

I looked at my companion in amazement.

"You think that is connected with these events, Pons?"

"Undoubtedly, Parker. It was what drew my attention to a number of significant factors. But I am hoping that my calls to Inspector Jamison at Scotland Yard and to Brother Bancroft will produce something pertinent."

He glanced up at the clock on the wall opposite.

"You must stay close to the Rectory from five o'clock onwards, Parker, if you would be so good."

"Certainly, Pons, if you think it necessary."

"It is vitally important. In fact, I would prefer you to deal with any visitors who may come to look at the books. Of course, our bait may not draw anyone this evening, but it is my experience that rare book collectors seldom miss such an opportunity. They usually descend in droves, sometimes within the hour of an advertisement appearing. I am relying on you, Parker."

"You may count on me, Pons. What will you be doing this afternoon?"

"Well, when I have taken the calls I am expecting I shall be off on a short tour of the district. I have a mind to visit one or two of the gypsy encampments in the neighbourhood."

"But you said that gypsies had nothing to do with it, Pons."

"That is perfectly correct. And it is just because gypsies are not connected with the affair that I wish to visit the camps."

I shrugged as Pons got up from the table.

"As you wish, Pons. But the matter still remains dark and impenetrable to me."

Solar Pons put his hand on my shoulder.

"Do not say so, Parker. Just keep your eyes and ears open and I am sure all will become clear before long."

His face became more grave.

"I must urge upon you, Parker, the seriousness of this business. The man who is after this fortune is ruthless and cunning. He will not become dangerous unless thwarted. Whoever calls this evening—whatever your suspicions—I must impress upon you the paramount importance of not giving him any inkling that his purposes are known."

"I understand, Pons. I must just give people the run of the library. But supposing our man takes that piece of paper from the Bible?"

Solar Pons shook his head impatiently.

"As I have already indicated, I am relying on him doing so, Parker. You must remain in the library, of course. And do try to give some intelligent answers about the books. There will undoubtedly be genuine dealers present. The most valuable books are in the locked glass bookcase near the far window. Only the genuine bibliophile will go there. The person who hangs about the shelves near the French windows will either be a cleric; an enthusiastic amateur who is interested in all old books as opposed to first editions; or the man we want. Just leave him alone. We shall know soon enough when that paper has been taken. He can do nothing until after dark, in any event."

"Certainly, Pons."

Solar Pons seemed satisfied and when he had called at the commercial office of the newspaper to thank the lady in charge of the files we left the building and took our taxi back to The Old Rectory. Pons' remarks about Miss Stuart's father had aroused many impressions in my mind; to tell the truth I had quite forgotten this aspect in the excitement of our discovery and with the passing of the hours toward the time when the newspaper advertisement would appear, my apprehension grew.

The roots of the mystery appeared to lie in happenings which had occurred ten or more years ago and the longer I thought about it the more impenetrable did the matter appear. Of course, I knew that the people who had robbed Cresswell Manor had apparently buried their booty in the church, but why the Rev. Stuart should die of shock in his library; or who the bearded man with the scarred thumb might be was beyond my poor capabilities. I tried to apply Pons' methods in my own humble way but soon had to give up.

And how had the coded messages appeared in the Rector's Bible in his own study? The more I thought about it the more tangled it became and it was with relief that I saw the lean, spare figure of Pons reappear in the garden after his walk. His carriage was alert and his eyes were sparkling as he came through the French windows into the library. He had earlier taken the two calls from Jamison and Bancroft Pons but had not volunteered any information and I knew better than to ask.

"Well, Parker," he said. "We progress."

"I am glad to hear it, Pons."

My companion sank into one of the wing chairs by the empty fireplace, now filled with a blaze of summer flowers, and stared at me quizzically.

"I think I not only know the reasons why Miss Stuart's bearded man appeared so frequently in this room, but I have his name."

I gazed at Pons open-mouthed.

"This is incredible, Pons."

"Pray do not exaggerate, Parker. Once I had the right direction in which to work it was merely a question of narrowing down."

He tented his thin fingers before him and fixed his gaze over toward the open French windows behind my back.

"Your walk has been productive, then?"

"It was not without its rewards, Parker. The exercise was certainly beneficial. Two of the sites were occupied by true Romanies. The third encampment, that in the quarry, was filled with a heterogeneous collection of *didikais* and travellers. It should serve our purpose well enough."

I glanced at Pons with rising irritation. He read the expression in my eyes and his lips curled in a faint smile.

"Just a few hours more, Parker. My theories are not proven yet."

He glanced over at the clock in the corner.

"And now, Parker, the time is almost six o'clock. Miss Stuart has her instructions. The housekeeper will refer any callers to you and you know my thoughts on the matter."

"Certainly, Pons."

Pons crossed over to the far bookshelves and checked the Bible we had replaced there. Then he closed and locked the French windows, shooting the bolts for good measure. He glanced round the room, as though setting the scene.

"Let me just recapitulate. The newspaper reaches Grassington in a quarter of an hour or a little after. If our man is as alert as I think him we might expect him as early as seven o'clock. Though he may not take the bait until tomorrow."

He crossed over toward the door.

"Oh, by the bye, any telephone calls you may regard as being from genuine dealers. Those in which the callers require appointments for tomorrow or succeeding days I should certainly class as bona fide and pass them on to Miss Stuart."

"Very well, Pons. What will you be doing?"

"I shall remain in my room, Parker, where I shall have a very good view of people walking up the front path without myself being observed. It would not do for our man to connect me with the energetic walker of this afternoon."

I could not repress a faint snort of impatience.

"Very well, Pons. No doubt this will all become clear in time."

"No doubt, Parker. I trust you to play your part."

Solar Pons quitted the room swiftly and I heard his quick, athletic tread on the stairs. He had no sooner closed the door of his chamber when I heard the shrill of the telephone from the hall outside. A few moments later the face of Hannah, the housekeeper, appeared nervously at the library door.

"Some London book dealers, sir. Shall I fetch Miss Stuart?"

I nodded and went to pick up the receiver.

"Brackett and Prall of Pall Mall here, sir," said the bland

voice at the other end. "Your advertisement in the *Surrey Observer* has been brought to our attention by a dealer in Guildford. Would it be convenient for us to arrange an appointment for tomorrow morning?"

I found Miss Stuart at my elbow and thankfully relinquished the instrument. I went back into the library and sat down at the table by the window. I attempted to read a book but I confess my mind was not on the lines. My purpose there in the library; the black mystery surrounding the death of our client's father; the bearded man who seemed to haunt the Rectory and grounds; the stolen hoard of silver buried in the church vault; and the responsibility Pons had placed upon me all combined to set my brain whirling.

I got up after a while and paced up and down the pleasant library, my mood widely at variance with the mellow sunlight which streamed through the windows. Twice more the telephone jangled in the hall outside and then Miss Stuart put her head round the door to say that two more rare book dealers hoped to come the following day.

It was almost seven o'clock when the front door-bell rang. I was just going out when Hannah crossed the hall in front of me, a tall, familiar figure behind her. He smiled somewhat crookedly at me.

"Ah, Dr. Parker, I saw the advertisement in the paper just now. Miss Stuart told me nothing about selling up her father's books."

"It was a sudden whim," I explained. "Please go in and browse about at your leisure."

"Thank you, doctor."

I watched Major Alan Kemp cross the hall with his firm, athletic stride and disappear within the study. I was about to join him when there came another ring at the door-bell. Hannah looked at me with widening eyes.

"Allow me this time," I said.

I opened the door to reveal the massive, bearded face of the Rector, the Rev. Isaac Stokesby. He wore a neat grey suit with his clerical collar beneath and he seemed considerably surprised to see me. He waved a copy of the *Surrey Observer* in my face.

"I have just seen Miss Stuart's advertisement, doctor. It seemed to me a good opportunity to add some ecclesiastical volumes to the church library. I trust it is not inconvenient . . . ?"

"By no means, Rector. Do come in. You know the study. You will find Major Kemp already there."

"Indeed," said Stokesby coolly.

He hesitated, as though he would have changed his mind, but apparently thought better of it.

"Perhaps you would be good enough to tell her I am here."

"I will tell Miss Stuart," I said.

When I returned with our client two other visitors had called; they were already in the study. I smiled encouragingly at Miss Stuart.

"It seems Mr. Pons' stratagem has proved effective, Dr. Parker."

I nodded.

"There is usually very sound method behind his even more extravagant actions, Miss Stuart. Will you join them in the library?"

"Let us both go, doctor."

"As you wish." As we entered the handsome room with the mellow rays of gold pouring in from the garden outside, the study seemed like nothing more than a public library. Two gentlemen in grey suits were examining volumes on the table and talking in hushed tones. The Rev. Stokesby had the locked bookcase open and was handling a leatherbound Bible reverently. I could not see the Major for a moment but then saw him up near the French windows where Pons and I had replaced the Bible with its corrupt texts.

Miss Stuart hurried forward and was soon engaged in animated conversation with her guests. I was about to join her when there came yet another ring at the front door. This time the caller was a small, dapper gentleman, impeccably dressed in a dark suit and wearing lavender-coloured gloves. He smiled amiably and searched in his pocket, as though looking for a card.

"Dear me, I seem to have forgotten them. Jethro Carpenter. Rare book dealer at your service. Would it be possible to view the collection mentioned in the advertisement?"

"By all means," I said. "Your colleagues are already in the library."

I led the way through and introduced the fifth man to the assembly. The room now seemed crowded and as the conversation proceeded I was able to study the other two men who had been admitted by Hannah.

One was a short, bearded man with a pronounced limp, named Judson Higgins. Though well dressed in expensive clothes and wearing white gloves, there was something sly and furtive in his appearance which I didn't take to. He had cold grey eyes beneath his whitening eyebrows and his thick hair was liberally dusted with silver. He had a high, mincing pedantic voice and was engaged in a shrill altercation with his companion.

This was a giant with red hair and a carefully trimmed moustache. He was about thirty-five years old and very strong and vigorous. But his eyes blinked mildly beneath his thick-lensed spectacles with tortoise-shell frames and he seemed more amused than otherwise at his colleague's comments on the quality of the books in the late Rector's library.

The Rev. Isaac Stokesby stood near Miss Stuart up near the empty fireplace, his dark eyes regarding the scene before him in an almost contemplative manner. The Major stood the other side of our client and seemed about to say something but was unable to gain her attention.

Jethro Carpenter contented himself with inclining his head to the company and then darted swiftly forward to the bookcase at the far end of the room, which I understood contained the rare volumes. I declined to join in the conversation but, mindful of Pons' stricture, tried to observe without appearing to take any notice.

I kept away from the bookcase near the window and as the housekeeper served coffee and biscuits to the guests an hour later, it was obvious that everyone in the room had had ample opportunity, at one time or another, to approach the Bible containing the message unobserved. The shelving was so arranged that it concealed the browser from the people standing near the fireplace; though that corner of the room was clearly in view from the French windows.

It was nearly nine o'clock before the last of the visitors had departed; no one else had come and it was with some relief that Miss Stuart and I exchanged glances as Hannah showed the last of the bibliophiles to the door. This was the Rector and I retained an impression of his sardonic, bearded face, the beard tinted with gold the dying sun as he hurried through the garden.

"Well, Dr. Parker," said our hostess gravely, as we re-entered the library, "I have several orders for books here and I only hope I shall be able to explain satisfactorily why they are not for sale when the would-be purchasers call again."

"I am afraid we have put you to some inconvenience, Miss Stuart. But I am sure Solar Pons would not have suggested this arrangement without good cause."

The girl flashed me a brief smile.

"I am certain you are right, Dr. Parker. Now, I think we have earned a glass of sherry."

She went over to pour while I unlocked and opened the French windows, letting sweet-scented air and the cheerful song of birds into the somewhat stuffy study. As I came back down the room I went to the Bible which was apparently the source of so much mystery and took it down from the shelf. I opened it and went through the slips of paper at the back. I felt a tingle of excitement as I re-examined them more thoroughly.

"Good heavens! The Bible verses are missing."

"I should be extremely disappointed if they were not, my dear fellow." Solar Pons was regarding me from the open study door, his eyes bright and alert. He rubbed his slender hands together as he came over to join us. Miss Stuart poured him a glass of sherry and we moved instinctively toward the dining room.

"Dinner will be served almost immediately, gentlemen," said our hostess. "I will not ask any further questions tonight. I hope you are hungry, as Hannah has prepared something special."

"We must do justice to it, Parker," said Solar Pons, his eyes twinkling over the rim of his glass. "We can do nothing till after dark but we must be in position not later than ten-thirty p.m."

Miss Stuart smiled wryly.

"Well, I do not know what you propose, Mr. Pons, but I drink most heartily to your success."

We all three raised our glasses.

8

I shifted my cramped position, my muscles cracking with the unwonted movement. Solar Pons put his hands to his lips in warning.

"We must just be patient, Parker. Our man is cunning and persistent. And he is extremely dangerous. You have your pistol?"

I nodded.

"You are certain he will come, Pons?" I whispered.

"I would stake my reputation on it, Parker. He has no reason for suspicion and we now know he has his hands on the thing he most covets."

"But will he read it aright, Pons?"

Pons smiled, glancing up at the moonlight which straggled through a stained glass window far above our heads. We crouched in the shadow of a large statuary group in the side-chapel of the church, facing the entrance. All was silent apart from the deep tick of the clock which told the passing of the hours. It was almost midnight and for the past hour the entire village of Grassington seemed to have been asleep. Not even the distant rumble of a passing motor vehicle had disturbed our vigil.

"Our man will read the message correctly, Parker. He knew what he was looking for before ever he came to The Old Rectory. It is hardly likely that he would not know the simple code employed."

I shook my head.

"Perhaps, Pons. But I must confess I am baffled. Any of

59

those people tonight could have been the man in question. But all of them had something suspicious about them if one read their actions a certain way."

Pons inclined his head.

"There is something of the eccentric in every collector of whatever type, Parker. It is endemic to the breed."

He broke off, his whole form rigid, his head forward in a listening attitude. I had heard nothing and opened my mouth to make some rejoinder when he stopped me by putting his hand on my arm. Then I heard what his sensitive ears had already caught. A faint creaking noise from somewhere far off in the church. It ceased and the silence resumed.

Pons moved over and put his mouth up against my ear.

"He has entered through a side door, Parker. An artist with a jemmy, evidently."

I eased my cramped legs and drew the pistol from my pocket, throwing off the safety-catch and laying it down carefully on the cool stone flags at my side.

"I am quite ready, Pons."

We waited for a few minutes more, sitting immobile, straining our ears to catch the slightest noise. Then I caught the scrape of a boot on the flagstones somewhere in the main body of the church.

I was unable to conceal a slight start at a vague shadow sliding through the moonlight which dappled the interior of the nave. I saw by Pons' expression that he had already noted it. I reached out silently and picked up the loaded revolver, holding it on my lap. My companion had his torch at the ready as the dark, stealthy figure drew nearer, moving with the utmost caution and circumspection. There was something almost obscene about this furtive intruder into this holy place at dead of night.

We both moved tighter into the wall in the deepest part of the shadow but our precautions were not needed; the figure that advanced through the chapel entrance on tip-toe, holding a slip of paper in its hand, was far too preoccupied to give more than a casual glance at his surroundings. He stopped still, as though deep in thought, and then turned toward us.

A shaft of moonlight spilling through the glass of one of the upper windows of the church fell clear upon his features and I could not repress a slight shudder. I felt Pons' fingers tighten on my arm and I lifted my pistol so as to be ready for any eventuality. The evil yellow face with the thick beard and burning eyes stared round menacingly and I understood for the first time what an ordeal Miss Stuart must have gone through.

I had no doubt in my own mind that this was the library intruder surprised by both her and her mother and the shock must have been severe indeed under the circumstances. Even here, with Pons at my side and the comforting feel of the revolver butt against my palm, the face exuded such menace that I felt the perspiration start out on my forehead.

The figure let fall an exclamation and then paced excitedly about, studying the flagstones. It went past the memorial to the children of which Pons had made so notable a use and then measured out the identical path already followed by my companion. The intruder knelt with another muffled gasp and I heard the chink of metal; then a low grating noise as he started to lever up the flagstone.

It was just at that moment that there came a loud noise at the main door of the church. Pons swore under his breath and let go of my arm. The crouching figure by the open hole in the chapel floor gave a convulsive leap into the air. It reached into its hip pocket as the beam of Pons' torch danced out to settle

61

on that horrific face. The man gave a snarl of rage and raised his hand.

"Quickly, Parker!" Pons snapped.

I was already on my feet, bringing the pistol up. I squeezed the trigger, the flash of flame from the muzzle seeming to light the church interior while the report echoed thunderously under the vaulting. I had aimed for the shoulder and my aim was true. The figure spun, clutching its left hand to its right forearm, and something clattered to the floor.

The front door of the church thundered back on its hinges as the bearded man blundered into some wooden chairs in the aisle. I was already racing after him but Pons was quicker still. Our quarry was up near the door when Pons brought him down with a running tackle. The two men landed asprawl at the feet of the gigantic Rector of Grassington, the Rev. Isaac Stokesby.

Eyes wide, he stared at the amazing tableau before him, while my torch beam continued to dance over the two struggling men on the floor. The Rector moved to a light switch and the interior of the church was filled with mellow radiance. The Rev. Stokesby's jaw dropped and his face was mottled with anger.

"Mr. Pons! Dr. Parker! What is this war-like intrusion into God's place?"

Pons got to his feet and dusted himself down. He gave a wry smile at the figure struggling in pain on the flagstones.

"Pray do not distress yourself, Rector," he said calmly. "God's will moves in mysterious ways, as the Bible says somewhere."

The Rector looked at my companion belligerently.

"That is all very well, Mr. Pons, but you will find this difficult to explain. There have been things going on here, as I told you, and I determined to keep watch. I noticed that you had abstracted the door key, which aroused my suspicions. Then tonight I saw your torch beam. I determined to wait until you came out to see what you were up to. But you were so long I decided to come in."

"Fortunate indeed that you waited, Rector," said Pons crisply. "This man was armed and desperate. And if you had run into him in the churchyard you would undoubtedly have scared him off."

He stepped back.

"Your department I think, Parker."

I knelt and made a cursory examination.

"A broken arm, Pons. Shock and loss of blood, of course. I can do little here."

Pons straightened up as I helped the bearded man to his feet and bound his wound with my handkerchief. All the fight seemed to have gone out of him. The Rector temporarily appeared to have been stricken speechless. As our prisoner's face came more fully into the light I could not resist an exclamation.

"Why, Pons, he is wearing a mask!"

Solar Pons chuckled.

"Is he not, Parker. Let us just have your views on his identity."

I had no hesitation.

"Why, Judson Higgins, the rare book dealer, Pons. He is about the same build and I noticed particularly that he wore gloves when he came to The Old Rectory last night."

I seized our prisoner's right hand and pointed out the misshapen white scar on the thumb. Solar Pons smiled at me encouragingly.

"Excellent, Parker. You will make a detective yet."

Without preamble he seized the bearded mask our prisoner

was wearing and tore it from him. I must confess I have never been so surprised or disappointed in my life. The face revealed was that of a complete stranger; a hard-faced, crop-headed man with battered features like a boxer, now reddened and perspiring from the constriction of the mask and the warmth of the evening. He kept his grey eyes sullenly on the floor. Pons' own eyes danced and he smiled at the Rector.

"If I am not much mistaken, Mr. Munro Slater, late of H.M. Prison, Dartmoor. Known to us as Jethro Carpenter, rare book dealer."

"But how was that possible, Pons?"

"Merely a clever make-up, Parker. And he was the only other of the book dealers who physically fits the bill. I have checked and Judson Higgins has a genuine limp."

He turned to the bearded churchman who was glaring impatiently at both of us.

"We owe you an explanation, Rector. We must first get this man to the local police. Then, if you are agreeable and despite the lateness of the hour, we must arouse Miss Stuart from her bed, and this matter must be settled once and for all."

9

"Coffee, Mr. Pons?"

Our client looked fresh and charming in her dressing gown and not like someone who had been awakened only half an hour before by the housekeeper in such a dramatic manner. It was half-past one in the morning but such was Pons' energy and vitality and such was our curiosity to hear the explanation for the weird business which had culminated so dramatically in the church that we took no heed of the time.

We sat at a round table at the far end of the study, the windows open to admit the sweet-scented night air, but with the curtains tightly drawn. The Rector, somewhat mollified, now that Pons had told him something of the circumstances, sat opposite drinking coffee while Pons and I were diagonally across from Miss Stuart presiding at the silver pot. Anyone who could have seen us at that hour would have found the sight decidedly strange.

Solar Pons put down his coffee cup and tented his fingers before him as he looked round the table with suppressed excitement.

"I am sorry to have roused you at such an inopportune hour, Miss Stuart, and what I am going to say may cause some distress."

Our client looked at us wide-eyed.

"Distress, Mr. Pons?"

Solar Pons nodded.

"It concerns your family and does not reflect very well on one of its members. Under these circumstances, if you would prefer the Rector to withdraw, I am sure he would understand."

Miss Stuart looked round the table in bewilderment, then clenched her jaw firmly.

"I have no secrets from the Rector, gentlemen. And I am sure that what is said here tonight will remain within these four walls unless there is good reason for making it public."

"Well said, Miss Stuart. I did not expect you to give any other answer."

Solar Pons looked at the fair-haired girl with a reassuring expression and sipped his coffee before replacing the cup in the saucer.

"This story begins a long time ago, Miss Stuart. In fact, it goes back to your childhood, one might say."

Miss Elizabeth Stuart looked at Pons wide-eyed.

"You astonish me, Mr. Pons."

My companion leaned back in his chair and began to light his pipe at our client's extended permission.

"As soon as you visited me at 7B Praed Street and told us your strange story, it was self-evident that your bearded visitor had a definite purpose in view. Two visits by the same burglar might be coincidence but a whole series, with nothing stolen, was so bizarre a circumstance that I rapidly came to the conclusion that the intruder was searching for something. Something hidden within this study."

Solar Pons put his match down in a crystal ash-tray on the table and puffed a cloud of fragrant blue smoke at the ceiling. He stared at it almost dreamily through the misty atmosphere.

"I had formed two conclusions before I left London, Parker. The first I have already mentioned. The second was that the man engaged in such a desperate search was disguised."

I looked at Pons in astonishment.

"You cannot mean it, Pons!"

My companion shook his head impatiently.

"It was self-evident, Parker. Miss Stuart had called the police. Inquiries had been made in the neighbourhood, on more than one occasion. But no one had seen a bearded man with an evil face and with a distinctive scar on his thumb. It was surely impossible for such a person to come and go in a small village like Grassington, even at night, without being seen. Therefore, it was elementary that he was disguised. As we have seen, our captive wore a mask. Not so much to conceal his own identity as to create a false one. So that even if he were seen it did not matter.

His scarred thumb could easily be concealed by gloves or a piece of sticking plaster whenever he went out in his own persona."

"That is all very well, Pons, and we now know the reason, but what was behind the whole charade?"

"Patience, Parker. The genesis of the affair goes back a good many years, and this is why we have to be discreet. It all began, Miss Stuart, in your childhood. Your uncle, Jeremy Stuart. You spoke of him as the black sheep of the family, if I recall your words correctly. And mentioned that he had emigrated to Australia. The expression black sheep usually carries the connotation of being a wild young fellow. Unfortunately, Jeremy Stuart was a habitual criminal and so far from emigrating he fled the country to avoid the police. In Australia he served a lengthy prison sentence for burglary and it was some years before England saw him again."

Miss Stuart had gone pale and she gazed at Pons with trembling lips. Pons put out his hand and clasped her own.

"Have no fear, Miss Stuart. Everything is over and done with. I am sorry to distress you but the truth must out, as I think the Rector would agree."

The Rev. Stokesby nodded sombrely. His burning eyes, which never left Pons' face, now wore an expression of approbation. The girl smiled faintly.

"I am sorry, Mr. Pons. It is a shock to find that an apparently respectable family contains such a hidden secret. But it explains much that was mysterious and troubled about my father."

I gave Miss Stuart an approving glance.

"It is no disgrace, Miss Stuart," I assured her. "Many families contain a member who goes wrong in one way or another. You are not responsible for your uncle and it is certainly not your family's fault that he turned out so badly."

"Well said, Parker," interjected Pons warmly. "And I am sure in his own way, Miss Stuart, your father did everything to redress the balance by his Christian work and charity in this parish."

"I can certainly endorse that, Mr. Pons," said the Rev. Isaac Stokesby. "I have never heard such testimony as the terms used by the people of Grassington about my predecessor."

Miss Stuart blushed.

"You are most kind, gentlemen. I promise I will not give way again, no matter what revelations you have to make about my uncle. Please proceed."

Solar Pons gave our client an encouraging look and went on as though he were thinking aloud.

"When your uncle eventually returned to England he sought refuge with his brother. It was while he was staying here at The Old Rectory that a daring scheme came into his mind. It was no less than the major robbery of valuables belonging to Sir Roger Cresswell of Cresswell Manor. He obviously carried it out with the aid of criminal associates. The gang escaped with valuables worth over £100,000. The haul would be worth considerably more now."

The Rector stared at Pons open-mouthed.

"How do you know all this, Mr. Pons?"

My companion shrugged.

"From my own deductions and the records of Scotland Yard. Friend Jamison has his uses, eh, Parker?"

"Undoubtedly, Pons. But I must confess I am in the dark over a number of things."

"Patience, Parker. It will take only a few minutes to unravel the remaining threads."

Pons turned to Miss Stuart.

"What do you remember of your uncle from your childhood, Miss Stuart?"

"He seemed very kind and amiable, Mr. Pons. He was very fond of antiquities and was often in the church and churchyard."

Solar Pons smiled.

"It was undoubtedly his researches in your church, Rector, which led him to the Cresswell vault."

"Eigh?"

The dark, bearded face looked startled.

"I am afraid, Mr. Stokesby, that you will find your church in some disorder tomorrow. Miss Stuart's uncle, when he committed the robbery at Cresswell Manor in 1912, had the foresight to prepare a hiding place no one would suspect. He hid the valuables in a hamper at the entrance to the Cresswell vault in the side chapel of the church. It has been there to this day and in fact Parker and I have only recently recovered it. This is what our visitor was looking for. Sir Roger Cresswell was killed on the Somme and buried in France and as he was the last of the line the vault was never opened again."

There was a thunderous silence in the study and the Rector stared at Solar Pons as though he had been struck dumb. Pons blew out more fragrant smoke and continued imperturbably.

"I do not know how closely he took his criminal associates into his confidence, but I am willing to bet that your uncle was the undisputed leader and told no one of the hiding place. He obviously prepared his groundwork well and secured the spoils at dead of night while your father and family were asleep. He could easily have taken the keys to the church from your father's study.

"The gang had scattered far and wide, of course, but Stuart, as the Rector's brother and a guest at The Old Rectory would have been above suspicion. From what I have been able to learn from Scotland Yard, your father quite naturally kept his brother's scandalous activities quiet. It is equally obvious that he did not really know anything about them, though he suspected much and at last came to realise his brother's callous and criminal nature. But Stuart is a common enough name and it is no great feat of reasoning to deduce that no one in Grassington would ever have known that their Rector's brother and honoured guest was in reality a hardened criminal who had served prison terms in Australia."

Pons got up and paced about as though impelled by the darting quicksilver of his thoughts.

"I am asking you to take a good deal on trust tonight, Miss Stuart, but I have no doubt at all that everything I am telling you is true in all but the most trivial detail."

"But how on earth did you know the late Rector's brother was involved, Pons?" I asked.

Solar Pons shook his head.

"It was the merest suspicion at first, Parker. It arose from a remark of Miss Stuart's regarding a quarrel between the brothers. I could not put a date to it at this distance in time but I became more and more convinced that the breach between the two men came about at the time of the Cresswell Manor affair. Jamison was invaluable here. He said that a convict named Jeremy Stuart had been suspected of the Manor robbery but the police had never been able to prove anything.

"It was while robbing a country house after leaving Grassington that he was caught by the police and sentenced to prison. The Governor at Dartmoor also mentioned Stuart and as I went over the chain of events and the dates, everything fitted. There was no doubt that Stuart for his part had kept his relationship with the Rector at Grassington a secret."

"In order that he could come back and collect the stolen property, Pons?"

"Naturally, Parker. And just in case anything went wrong he left a clue to its location on a slip of paper in the old Bible in the study here. He undoubtedly read that Sir Roger had been killed and buried in France and realised the vault had never been opened."

Pons again pulled out the sheet with the enigmatic verses and passed them across to Miss Stuart and the Rector. He briefly enumerated the code and pointed out the message he had deciphered.

"All this explains the painful events on that night two years ago when your father met his death, Miss Stuart. We are unlikely to know now the precise reason Stuart came back. He had escaped from Dartmoor and was at liberty for several months. He may have returned to Grassington for the hidden valuables; more likely to take refuge with the brother he hoped would not refuse him the Christian charity he had always found."

Miss Stuart gazed at Pons, her lower lip trembling.

"That was why Daddy...?" she began.

"A heart attack through shock," Pons said quietly. "I cannot prove it but I am certain your father was near the window and had actually picked up that very Bible, all unconscious of the message hidden within it. The shock of seeing his brother, an escaped convict, at the window was too much for him. Not only that but the disgrace his wife and daughter would have to face if the scandal ever came out. He had forbidden his brother ever to set foot in the house again and here he was, probably

71

with the police hot at his heels. His heart was weak and he collapsed and died. The expression on his face, which you described so graphically, Miss Stuart, is common in cases of sudden death from heart failure, as you have already indicated, Parker."

"Just so, Pons. But how do you arrive at this conclusion?"

"With the aid of friend Jamison. Prompted by me he did some research in the criminal records. The Dartmoor escape of Stuart took place just two days before the Rector died under such tragic circumstances. And brother Bancroft and the present Governor of Dartmoor have been most helpful. Stuart was recaptured some time afterwards, in the London area, and returned to the Moor."

"But what has all this to do with the man, Munro Slater, Pons?"

"I am coming to that, Parker, if you will give me time," returned Pons reprovingly.

He turned back to our client.

"So here we have a rascally brother; stolen money hidden in the church of a devout and admirable Rector; the good brother unfortunately dead; a set of clues to the location of the Cresswell Manor haul hidden in the Bible in the study; and a complete stranger searching for it. What does that suggest to you, Parker?"

I pondered for a moment, my eyes on the ceiling.

"Why, that Jeremy Stuart could not come himself, Pons."

Solar Pons chuckled.

"Excellent, Parker. You constantly astonish me and are becoming a credit to my training."

He ticked off points on his fingers.

"Let us just recapitulate briefly. The bearded intruder who haunted The Old Rectory had one interest only, the library.

He appeared to favour only one portion of the library shelving. That led us to the Bible with its hidden message. I immediately seized on the simple code which led us to the church and to the hidden valuables. They bore the arms of the Cresswells. The newspaper account gave us the details of the robbery, the date and so forth. A call to Bancroft and Jamison furnished me with all the background information. You have said just now that Jeremy Stuart could not come for the money himself, Parker. He is dead, unfortunately, or perhaps, in view of the distress he caused Miss Stuart's family, fortunately would be a more appropriate term."

There was a deep silence. I stared at Solar Pons, taking in the lean, alert features and the sparkle in his eyes.

"He died in prison, Pons?"

Solar Pons nodded.

"Exactly, Parker. In Dartmoor a year ago. But before he died in the prison infirmary he imparted his secret to another member of the gang, Munro Slater."

"I see, Pons. And Munro Slater has only just been released from prison."

"Not quite, Parker. Last winter. But the manifestations at The Old Rectory began just a few weeks after his release."

"This is remarkable, Mr. Pons," put in the Rev. Stokesby. His face wore an expression of amiability, the first I had seen since we had made his acquaintance.

"But why did Stuart simply not tell Slater where the material was buried, Pons?"

Solar Pons shook his head.

"Stuart had had a stroke. He might well have recovered. He was cunning to the end. Besides, there was a nurse at the bedside. He was able only to articulate to his companion in crime the address and the fact that he must look in a Bible in the study. I had that from Slater himself at the police station. He has decided to confess everything."

"But there had been no strangers in the vicinity, Pons?" I objected. "Particularly men with beards."

Solar Pons held up his hand.

"I would not have expected there to be, Parker. The beard was an obvious disguise. There remained the scar on the thumb as described by Miss Stuart but that could easily have been hidden in a number of ways; by gloves, a bandage or even as our man masquerading as a workman, with his hand smeared with paint. I had to look elsewhere. You may remember I showed interest in gypsy bands in the neighbourhood. I had a most illuminating walk in the district yesterday. Two of the camps were occupied by genuine Romanies. I discounted them immediately."

I looked at Pons with a puzzled expression.

"Why so, Pons?"

"For the simple reason that the world of the real Romany is the most exclusive and hermetically sealed there is. No one in those circles would admit a stranger to their midst. My attention was immediately drawn to the only remaining encampment in the area, that occupied by travellers, tinkers and other itinerants. A little money soon obtained me the information I needed. I met one of the scrap-dealers along the road. He told me of a man who had come among them some months earlier and who paid rent for an empty caravan. His food was fetched from the village and he seldom went out. I realised I should have to provide some bait to bring him to my hook and drafted the advertisement for the newspaper, with the result we have seen."

Miss Stuart smiled and gazed at Pons with undisguised admiration.

"It is amazing, Mr. Pons. I do not know how to thank you."

Solar Pons chuckled.

"It has been reward enough, taking such a pleasant holiday in Grassington in such admirable weather. But I fear we must break things short and return to town tomorrow. Jealousy is one of the major passions and I should not like to risk a confrontation with the Major . . . "

The girl blushed a becoming pink and the Rector's teeth glinted whitely in his beard.

"I do not know what you mean, Mr. Pons."

Solar Pons glanced at me, his eyes dancing.

"I think you do, Miss Stuart. The Major's admiration for you is undisguised and I would not like to think my presence here would give him cause to fear a rival."

He moved toward the door.

"We will make arrangements tomorrow to get the Cresswell valuables back to their rightful owners, though as the line has died out they may be regarded by a Coroner's Court as treasure trove."

"In that case I think Father would wish me to share the money with the church," said Miss Stuart, turning to the Rector with a ready smile.

"Well, well, Parker, it would appear that poetic justice has been done," said Solar Pons. "In the meantime a good night's sleep would not come amiss before facing the rigours of the metropolis."

THE ADVENTURE OF THE
SINGULAR SANDWICH

∂ 1

"GREAT HEAVENS, PONS! My old friend involved in murder! It cannot be true!"

I put down the paper in utter consternation and turned to my companion in astonishment. The heading in *The Times* and the accompanying account was completely shattering and I found myself unable to speak for some moments after my initial outburst.

Solar Pons stirred sympathetically at the other side of the breakfast table, his deep-set eyes searching my face. It was a damp, muggy morning in early April with a fitful sun penetrating the mist and spilling into our sitting-room at 7B Praed Street.

I passed him the newspaper, still too moved to speak. Pons took it, his eyes fixed intently on my face. He pulled at the lobe of his left ear, his features a mask of concentration as he spread the paper out on the table by the side of his plate.

"This business of the portrait painter? I did not know you knew Aramis Tregorran."

"We were at medical school together, Pons, until he abandoned medicine for a career in art. That it should come to this!"

Pons read the item, his thin fingers tense with excitement.

"It would appear that Mr. Tregorran has got himself into deep waters, Parker," he said eventually.

"I had been inclined to envy him his success, Pons," I said somewhat bitterly. "I see now that I have done better to stick to medicine."

Solar Pons glanced at me ironically.

"I would not say that your life has been unsuccessful, my dear fellow. But then Tregorran's career has been too spectacular for most of us to emulate. And his descent has been equally swift, it would appear."

I took the newspaper from him and studied the heading of the story again. It was unbelievable.

The item read:

FAMOUS PORTRAIT PAINTER CHARGED
WITH MURDER
ARAMIS TREGORRAN ACCUSED OF
STRANGLING WIFE.

The article, from *The Times'* own correspondent, described a bizarre state of affairs at Tregorran's Chelsea studio.

It appeared that the previous afternoon his servant had been aroused by screams and choking noises from the studio at the top of his house. Alarmed, he had rushed to the door but had been unable to make anyone hear. The door had been locked and he had to break it in.

He had found a unique scene of horror. The whole studio was a shambles with furniture overturned and canvases tipped awry. Aramis Tregorran himself had been slumped unconscious in the middle of the floor, in a muddle of trampled paint-tubes. At the far side of the room, near the big window letting in the northern light, Mrs. Sylvia Tregorran was lying dead, manually strangled.

When brought to consciousness, Tregorran had been incoherent and unable to make sense to his manservant, Relph, or the housekeeper, Mrs. Mandeville.

The police had been called and later last night Tregorran, who had been taken to Chelsea Police Station, had been charged with murder.

"Hullo, Pons," I said as I reached the end of the story in the paper, "I see that our friend Jamison is in charge of the case."

"I had already observed that, Parker," observed my companion drily.

"On this occasion, however, it would appear that he is right when he avers that the matter is a plain case of a domestic quarrel ending in murder."

I shook my head sadly.

"I still cannot believe it, Pons."

Solar Pons looked at me sympathetically.

"Such things are always difficult to believe, Parker. Especially when such tragedies happen to old friends."

I turned back to the newspaper and studied the narrative again.

"I had heard, Pons, that Tregorran was not on the best of terms with his wife, but from what I know of his character he would not hurt a mouse. He was the gentlest of men."

Pons got up from his chair, took a spill from the fireplace and lit his pipe. He spiralled a column of blue smoke toward the ceiling of our sitting-room. Then he came back to sit in his chair and looked at me interrogatively.

"What you are trying to tell me, my dear fellow, is flying in the face of the evidence," he said gently.

"Nevertheless, I would feel easier in my mind if you would look into the affair, Pons."

Solar Pons had surprise in his eyes.

"You cannot be serious, Parker. I have not been consulted in the matter."

"But if I asked you, Pons?"

Solar Pons smiled thinly and pulled reflectively at the lobe of his left ear. "That would be entirely different, Parker. I could not, of course, ignore such a request from such a close friend and companion. Just hand me that newspaper again, will you?"

He took it from me and sat smoking and studying it for the next ten minutes in silence. He put it down and sat staring at the flickering flames in the fireplace.

"It is true that Inspector Jamison is not the most brilliant of police officers but I must confess that my own faculties are considerably rusted this morning."

"What do you mean, Pons?"

"I overlooked an obvious anomaly when reading this account, unless the newspaper has made a mistake."

"What do you mean, Pons?"

"The door, Parker. It was locked."

I looked at him in surprise.

"What of it, Pons?"

"It is surely unusual for a man to lock his studio door in his own house, particularly during the lunch-hour."

"I did not read that, Pons."

"Obviously, Parker, but there is only one implication to be drawn if the servant had to break the door in. The key was not in the lock. Therefore it had to be on the other side."

"Perhaps he wished a private interview with his wife and during the quarrel rage overcame him?"

"Perhaps, Parker. But we do not even know there was a quarrel. That must await my own questions to your Mr. Tregorran."

"Excellent, Pons! I would feel so much happier if you would just give us the benefit of your immense skill in these matters."

"Flattery, Parker, flattery!"

But Solar Pons had a twinkle in his eyes as he said the words. Before he could say anything else there was a ring at the bell, a muffled conversation in the hall below and the tread of feet ascending the stairs. A few moments later there came a deferential tap at the door and the good-natured features of our amiable landlady, Mrs. Johnson, were thrust into the room.

"Inspector Jamison to see you, Mr. Pons!"

"Thank you, Mrs. Johnson. A cup of coffee, Inspector? There is still plenty in the pot."

"Thank you, Mr. Pons."

The somewhat deflated figure of Jamison sank into the chair proffered by Pons. He took the coffee-cup I held out to him with a grateful expression on his features.

Pons doffed his old grey dressing-gown and took up his jacket from the back of a chair in a corner. He looked at our visitor with an alert expression in his deep-set eyes.

"It is some while since we last met officially, Jamison. That little business of Romane Schneider, was it not?"

The Scotland Yard man put down his cup in the saucer with a faint chink in the silence of our sitting-room.

"This is a little different to that, Mr. Pons," he said with a smirk. "In fact I would not be here at all if it were not for an urgent plea by Mr. Aramis Tregorran's solicitor."

"Strange that you should seek my advice in another artistic matter, Inspector. First a sculptor, now a painter."

Pons looked at me with a little mischievous smile of enjoyment playing about his mouth. Inspector Jamison seemed discomfited but he nevertheless took another sip of the coffee before replying.

"Not at all, Mr. Pons. It's the clearest-cut case of murder I've ever seen. You've no doubt come to the same conclusion if you've read this morning's paper."

"Why are you here, then?"

"Because of this urgent request by the accused's solicitor, Mr. Pons. And because Tregorran specially asked Dr. Parker to seek your advice. He swears he is innocent. It is ridiculous, of course, but I would not like it to be thought that the Yard had not given him every chance. And as your name was mentioned . . ."

"Of course, Inspector. You are noted for fairness," murmured Solar Pons blandly.

He took a turn about the fireplace, the blue smoke from his pipe making little eddying whorls around his lean, dynamic figure. He came back to stand in front of the Inspector.

"All the same you are not certain, are you?"

Jamison shifted uncomfortably in his chair.

"To tell the truth there are one or two odd points," he mumbled.

"Exactly," said Solar Pons crisply. "The small matter of the key to the studio for example."

Jamison stared at Pons in amazement.

"How on earth did you know that, Mr. Pons?"

"It was self-evident if *The Times* report had any accuracy. And it is not usual to find *The Times* slack in such particulars."

Jamison scratched his head.

"You are right, Mr. Pons. We could not find the key at all."

"Yet the door had to be broken in?"

"Exactly."

Solar Pons looked at me with a little smile of triumph.

"Nevertheless, things look extremely black for Mr. Tregorran, doctor," continued the Inspector, noting the look of relief on my face. "I should not get up your hopes too high."

"Where is Mr. Tregorran at this moment, Jamison?" asked my companion.

"At Chelsea Police Station, still being questioned, Mr. Pons. He has been detained overnight, of course."

Pons inclined his head.

"Naturally."

I turned to Jamison.

"I trust that my friend has been afforded every facility to contact his friends and legal advisers."

Jamison gave a short, barking laugh.

"You may be sure of that, doctor. Would I be here otherwise? And I have already allowed him to see his solicitor."

"You have made your point, Jamison," said Solar Pons. "There is no complaint on that score."

"You will come then, Mr. Pons?"

"Most certainly, though if you have been unable to unravel the matter, it is extremely unlikely that my humble efforts in the same capacity would do better."

"You are making sport of me, Mr. Pons."

"Only a little, Inspector," said Pons with a thin smile.

"But first I have a fancy to see the scene of the murder. We will visit Chelsea Police Station afterwards, if you please."

"As you wish, Mr. Pons. The studio is just as we found it, though the body has been removed, of course."

My companion turned to me.

"Are you free, Parker?"

"Certainly, Pons, if you require me. It is my rest day."

"That is settled, then. Lead on, Inspector."

2

Tregorran's house turned out to be one of those modest-looking white-painted, flat-chested houses in which Chelsea abounds, set back in a cobbled mews. Like most houses of its type its unassuming three-storey exterior concealed large, gracious rooms and unostentatiously displayed wealth. As we alighted from Jamison's police vehicle, Pons walked over to the minuscule front garden, set back behind blue-painted railings, and raked the façade of the building with his keen, penetrating eyes.

Watched silently by myself and the Inspector he passed through an archway at the side and glanced up at a staircase which led to an outside door at the top of the steps.

"That is the studio?"

"That is so, Mr. Pons. Mr. Tregorran had it built so in order that his sitters and other clients could come and go without disturbing the household."

"Eminently practical."

Pons stood in deep thought, his hand pulling at the lobe of his right ear as I had so often seen him.

"I have a mind to look at the scene of the crime without disturbing the household either. Is that practicable?"

"Certainly, Mr. Pons. The door is unlocked and there is a constable on duty."

We followed the Inspector up the steps and found ourselves in front of a glassed-in porch. The inner door gave on to a small lobby in which the main entrance of the studio was set.

"There is no key to the outer door of the porch, Mr. Pons," Jamison volunteered. "And so far as Mr. Tregorran is concerned, never has been."

"I see."

Solar Pons stepped forward as Jamison opened the polished mahogany interior door. He stood frowning at the bronze key in the obverse side of the lock.

"Is this key normally in the lock?"

Jamison looked surprised.

"No, Mr. Pons. It is Mr. Tregorran's own key which he usually keeps on his desk. This door is usually kept locked unless he is expecting visitors."

"I see. That seems clear enough."

Pons bent to examine the lock and then straightened up, closing the door behind him. We found ourselves in an extremely elegant, luxuriously furnished studio, the watery sun spilling down through the massive skylight windows.

An alert, fresh-faced police constable in uniform came down the room toward us, evident pleasure on his features. Solar Pons smiled.

"Ah, Constable Mecker. It is good to see you again."

"Thank you, sir. The pleasure is mutual, I am sure. This is a bad business. I am sorry, Dr. Parker. I understand the accused gentleman is a friend of yours."

"That is correct, Mecker," I said. "Though Mr. Pons here hopes to clear the matter up."

There was regret in Mecker's eyes as he shook his head, turning back to my companion.

"Begging your pardon, sir, even your great skill will find it a well-nigh impossible task to complicate such a simple matter."

"Well, if somewhat deprecatingly put, Mecker," said Solar Pons drily. "So your superior has been telling me. We shall just have to wait upon events. And now I must set to work."

He went across the studio, which was in a shocking state with tumbled furniture and canvases scattered about.

"This door has not been touched?"

"Our people went over it for finger-prints, Mr. Pons, but it is substantially as we found it."

Pons went down on his knees and carefully examined the shattered lock.

"Hullo!"

There was surprise in his voice.

"The key is in the lock!"

"Impossible, Mr. Pons!"

"Just look for yourself, Jamison."

I crossed over to stand behind the Inspector as he stooped to the door, which was off its hinges and lying propped against the wall. Jamison's jaw dropped blankly.

"You are right, Mr. Pons."

A bronze key, similar to that in the studio entrance door, was protruding from the brass lock-plate.

"You are sure it could not have been overlooked?"

Little spots of red stood out on Jamison's cheeks.

"Positive, Mr. Pons. We made a careful check. That is so, is it not, Constable Mecker?"

"Certainly, sir."

The puzzlement of his superior was echoed in Mecker's own eyes.

"Well, well. This is most interesting."

Solar Pons straightened up and rubbed his thin hands together in satisfaction.

"This is a most important development. I commend it to you, Inspector."

I saw the puzzlement in Jamison's eyes but said nothing, merely watched Pons as he went about the room in the brisk, alert manner I had grown to know so well. At a sign from the Inspector Mecker went to stand by the far door, out of earshot.

"Where was Mrs. Tregorran found?"

"Over here, Mr. Pons. She had been manually strangled and our doctor's post mortem report confirms this. She was a well-built and perfectly healthy woman, some thirty-eight years old."

Pons nodded and walked over to a place beneath one of the great skylights at the far side of the studio. From the jumble of broken picture frames and a crack in the glass where one of the panes extended almost to the floor, it was evident that a savage struggle had taken place. Pons had his powerful pocket lens out now and went minutely over the carpet and surroundings in this corner of the studio.

He straightened up, dusting the knees of his trousers.

"I can learn nothing further here."

He stood looking down with a faint frown of puzzlement on his features.

"They had no children?"

Jamison shook his head.

"No, Mr. Pons."

He hesitated slightly, embarrassment on his face.

"From what the servants tell us they were a quarrelsome couple. Begging your pardon, Dr. Parker. The marriage had gone wrong but apparently Tregorran had sought a reconciliation. He was painting Mrs. Tregorran's picture at the time of her death."

"Indeed?"

The puzzlement on Solar Pons' face had increased.

"Where is this portrait?"

"It is on the easel yonder, Mr. Pons."

"Hmm. So apparently Mrs. Tregorran was in the studio here, having her portrait painted, the couple on reasonably good terms, if I read the situation aright?"

"That would appear to be the case, Mr. Pons," said the Inspector, shifting heavy-footed from one leg to the other. "We have various statements from the servants..."

"We will get to them later, Jamison, if you please..." said Pons brusquely.

He turned to me.

"That seems rather odd, Parker, does it not?"

I nodded.

"The painting of the portrait, Pons? It certainly seems so to me. I had heard that the Tregorrans did not get on well together, but did not feel it was my place to point it out to you."

Solar Pons stared at me with a languid expression on his face.

"Perfectly correct, Parker. You were old friends and you left me to form my own impressions. Exactly as I should have done had the position been reversed."

He walked softly over to the easel indicated by Jamison. It stood directly beneath the main skylight and just across from it, on a raised platform, was the chair so fatally vacated by the sitter. Paint-brushes were scattered on the floor, near a paint-bespattered palette and there was a sharp, chemical smell in the air. On a small side-table was a half-empty bottle of lager, with the stopper and foil lying by its side; an empty beer glass; and on a blue plate, the partly consumed remains of a sandwich. Jamison had approached and answered Pons' unspoken question.

"He was in the habit of eating snacks in the studio all the while he was working."

"I see."

Pons stood plunged in thought, his keen eyes darting from easel to the scattered mess on the floor and then across to the dais. We waited silently while he made a minute examination. While he was doing this I looked at the almost completed canvas. It depicted a beautiful, imperious-looking woman with long blonde hair who stared insolently at the viewer from very frank, blue eyes. Jamison intercepted my glance.

"Lovely woman, wasn't she, doctor? But a firebrand from what I can gather."

I waited until Pons had rejoined me and he stood staring at the canvas in silence.

"It seems fairly clear what happened," he said at last. "Tregorran put down the glass here and resumed his painting. At some period he dropped the palette, brushed past the easel—there are some threads of blue cloth caught on a protruding nail here—and rushed across to the dais. Mrs. Tregorran thrust back her chair—the indentations in the carpet on the dais where the sitter's chair normally stood are plain enough to see—and fled toward the door leading to the house. Tregorran intercepted her and penned her in the corner, where he strangled her among the picture-frames. In my judgement the attack was ferocious and unpremeditated. Both circumstances are singular."

"Why so, Pons?"

Solar Pons smiled a thin smile.

"For obvious reasons, Parker. One, you have already told me that Tregorran was the gentlest of men, who would not harm a fly. But this attack was savage and brutal. That it was un-premeditated is equally obvious. The man was consuming his lunch and painting in an apparently ordinary manner when he was so overcome by rage that he rushed over toward his sitter and attacked and murdered her."

"It is extraordinary, Pons," I said, "and I do not pretend to understand it. Perhaps they had an argument and Mrs. Tregorran said something so insulting that it set him off?"

Solar Pons' eyes were bright as he stared at the canvas.

"Perhaps," he said softly. "We shall see."

He turned back to the Inspector.

"I should like to question the servants next."

"By all means, Mr. Pons."

It was with some relief that we quitted the heavy atmosphere of the studio, Mecker ushering us through the gaping opening which now led into the house. We found ourselves in a wide cor-ridor, hung with gold-framed pictures by Tregorran and broken at intervals by a series of low mahogany bookcases. There was a small octagonal table outside the door and Pons' sharp eyes flickered over it. A lamp stood on it, but the top was a little dusty and I saw my companion stoop and frown at the square line which divided the dusty and dusted segment of the table.

"Something normally stands here, Jamison."

The thin form of the Inspector gave an expressive shrug.

"Tregorran didn't like to be disturbed while he was working, Mr. Pons. The servants were in the habit of leaving trays of food for him here."

"I see. And the person responsible was getting a little careless in the dusting up here."

"So it would seem, Mr. Pons."

Pons stood in silence a moment longer before swivelling to look back at the corridor behind him. To Jamison's evident astonishment he walked back to the end of the passage. It turned at right angles. There was a small, square entry with a single widow.

The weak sun glimmered at the panes and glittered on the brass handle set in the panelling. Pons turned it and stepped through. We found ourselves once again back in the glassed-in porch. The door through which we had entered was panelled on the other side and looked from the lobby just as though it were a solid wall, the edges of the door fitting cunningly behind the beading.

Solar Pons smiled at me.

"Interesting, is it not, Parker?"

Inspector Jamison scratched his head.

"Two entrances from the house to the studio. This needs looking into, Mr. Pons."

Solar Pons pulled reflectively at the lobe of his left ear.

"On the other hand it may have a perfectly obvious explanation."

"In what way, Mr. Pons?"

"Convenience, Jamison. We are on the first floor. It looks a long way back down to the front door. If Tregorran had his studio entrance here it might be just as convenient for his servants and guests to go out this way as well from time to time."

"Perhaps, Mr. Pons. But why the concealed entrance?"

Solar Pons smiled again.

"That explanation is equally simple. Entrance to the studio is one thing. But Tregorran would not wish to advertise an entrance into the main house to burglars."

"That is so, Pons," I put in. "But another explanation has suggested itself to you?"

"You excel yourself, Parker. Let us say, another possibility. I commend that to your ratiocinative instincts, Jamison."

He led the way back into the main house again and we made our way down a handsome carved pine staircase into the entrance hall. Here a tall, thin man with careworn features was waiting for us, an elderly woman, evidently the housekeeper, standing at his side.

"There is nothing to be alarmed about," said Jamison as we came down the last flight.

"This is Mr. Solar Pons. He is here to help Mr. Tregorran."

The worried expression on the manservant's face deepened as he came forward.

"This is a dreadful business, Mr. Pons."

"Indeed, Relph. You are Mr. Tregorran's valet, I understand?"

"General factotum, Mr. Pons. Valet-butler to be precise. This is Mrs. Mandeville, the housekeeper."

Pons acknowledged the introduction gravely.

"Let us go inside somewhere and sit down, Jamison. It will be much more conducive to comfort and efficiency."

"By all means, Mr. Pons."

Relph opened a sliding door at one side of the hall and led the way into a handsome, bow-fronted room with cream walls, containing a good deal of Regency furniture. My companion prevailed upon Relph and Mrs. Mandeville to sit opposite us on a divan while Jamison went to stand by the carved pine fireplace, his eyes fixed on the low fire flickering on the hearth. Solar Pons lit his pipe, the match-head rasping against the box unnaturally loudly in the silence which had fallen on the room. His deep-set eyes surveyed the two servants piercingly.

"I would like you both to tell me, in your own words, exactly what you know about yesterday's occurrences."

Relph glanced interrogatively at the housekeeper, who stirred and licked her lips. She spoke first, glancing occasionally at her colleague, as though for corroboration.

"I do not know that there is much to tell in my case, Mr. Pons. Mr. Tregorran breakfasted as usual yesterday morning and I did not see him again. He took a tray at lunch-time and there was a disturbance at about two o'clock. I ran out into the hall and then Mr. Relph told me what had happened. I am still stunned, Mr. Pons."

"Quite so," said Solar Pons soothingly. "And Mrs. Tregorran?"

"I do not understand, Mr. Pons."

"She had been estranged from her husband, had she not?"

Once again an uneasy glance passed from the housekeeper to Relph.

"I do not see that it is my place, Mr. Pons . . . "

Solar Pons tented his fingers before him and looked at Mrs. Mandeville steadily.

"Those are admirable sentiments and ones ideal in a housekeeper, but we are dealing with a murder inquiry."

The smooth, motherly face flushed.

"Yes, that is quite true, Mr. Pons. Mr. and Mrs. Tregorran had had some terrible rows and she had gone to live elsewhere. We were all surprised to hear that they were together again."

"I see."

Solar Pons was silent for a moment, his eyes fixed steadily

somewhere up over the fireplace, as though he saw things denied to us.

"How did this come about?"

"I do not quite know, Mr. Pons. I think Mr. Relph knows more about it, being in Mr. Tregorran's confidence, you see. But I understood he was painting his wife's portrait, which amazed us all."

Solar Pons nodded, putting the stem of his now extinct pipe between his strong, yellow teeth.

"When did Mrs. Tregorran arrive yesterday?"

"In the morning, Mr. Pons. Mr. Relph was upstairs somewhere and the two maids were otherwise occupied, so I answered the door myself."

"How did she seem?"

"Quite normal. Perfectly pleasant, in fact. I showed her upstairs and then Mr. Relph appeared and took her through to the studio."

"I see. Thank you Mrs. Mandeville. You have been most helpful."

"If you wish Tregorran's statement, I have it here, Mr. Pons," Jamison volunteered from his position near the fireplace. He fumbled in his breast pocket and came up with a set of official-looking papers.

Pons shook his head.

"Thank you, no, Jamison. I prefer to question my client without any preconceived ideas. I may glance at that later."

"As you wish, Mr. Pons."

Jamison frowned at me and put the docket back in his pocket, evidently disgruntled.

Pons turned back to Relph.

"What have you to add?"

The manservant was evidently under some constraint, for he fidgeted a little before replying.

"As Mrs. Mandeville says, gentlemen, Mr. Tregorran kept to the studio most of the morning. I had some conversation with him through the door and he informed me that his wife would be arriving for a sitting. He had been working on her portrait for the past fortnight."

Pons' eyes were keen as he tamped fresh tobacco into the bowl of his pipe.

"Was that usual, Mr. Tregorran speaking with the door between you like that?"

"Quite usual, sir. Mr. Tregorran did not like to be disturbed while he was working."

"Even though he had no model there?"

The manservant nodded.

"There was a deal of preparatory work, Mr. Pons. And Mr. Tregorran had many other commissions."

"I see. Pray continue."

"Mrs. Tregorran arrived a little before eleven o'clock. As Mrs. Mandeville has said, I escorted her to the studio and after tapping on the door announced her arrival."

"Did you see Mr. Tregorran on that occasion?"

"No, Mr. Pons. I left Mrs. Tregorran at the door and as I gained the end of the corridor I heard the door close behind her. I was busy about my household duties and at about midday I collected a tray from Mrs. Mandeville and took him an early lunch. I knocked at the door and left the tray on the table outside the door."

"That was a usual procedure also, I understand?"

"Indeed, sir."

"And Mrs. Tregorran?"

"The lady rarely took lunch, sir; or if she did she ate at about two o'clock in the afternoon. But Mr. Tregorran's eating habits were entirely different and he often said he felt starved if he did not take something at midday."

"I see. What then?"

"Nothing untoward occurred, sir, until shortly after two o'clock. Mrs. Tregorran was still in the studio and I was in my room, reading after lunch. I was just about to return to my duties when I heard terrible screams coming from the direction of the studio. My room is just along the corridor, around the corner, but the noise was so horrible that I could hear it clearly from there. I ran down to the door but as I had expected, it was locked."

Solar Pons' eyes were sharp and glittering as he lit his pipe, shovelling aromatic blue smoke over his shoulder.

"Pray be precise as to detail. It is most important."

"Very well, Mr. Pons. There was no reply to my agitated knocking. The screaming had stopped but I could hear a fierce struggle taking place in the studio. Things were being knocked over and bodies were blundering about. It was a dreadful time and difficult to describe, I am afraid."

"Your account is admirably clear, Relph. What then?"

"Other members of the staff had appeared, including Mrs. Mandeville. She sent a maid for the gardener and he and I broke the door in together. I went into the room alone, and as a result of what I saw the gardener went immediately to summon the police. Mrs. Tregorran was lying near one of the big windows, her eyes wide open and staring, her tongue protruding from her mouth. It was evident that she had been strangled, for there were heavily indented bruise-marks on her throat."

"Where was Mr. Tregorran?"

"He was slumped in a heap in the centre of the studio, sir, midway between the platform used by the models, and the window. He was in a dreadful state, his face white and chalky, perspiration on his forehead, his eyes glazed."

"Did he give you any explanation as to why he had attacked his wife?"

The manservant shook his head.

"He was incapable of saying or doing anything, Mr. Pons. He was incoherent, barely conscious and in a complete state of collapse. He kept mumbling things. In fact, had I not known Mr. Tregorran so well, I should have said he was little short of a madman."

There was a deep silence in the room. Solar Pons looked at me, his eyes shrewd and penetrating.

"Most singular, Parker, is it not?"

"Indeed, Pons," I said.

My companion rose to his feet.

"Well, there is little further to be learned here unless you have anything to add, Relph. You have been most helpful."

Relph shook his head.

"I have told you everything I know, sir."

He looked resentfully at Inspector Jamison

"Unless you wish to know personal matters that might tell against Mr. Tregorran. Such as those the Inspector questioned me about."

"Oh, what was that, Inspector?"

Jamison shifted uncomfortably by the fireplace.

"We're seeking information about certain lady friends of Mr. Tregorran's, Mr. Pons."

Relph had a stubborn, defiant look on his face.

"My answer would be the same to you, sir, as to the Inspector here."

"And what was that?"

"Why, to ask Mr. Tregorran, sir."

Pons chuckled.

"Quite right. Your attitude does you credit. Come, Parker. It is time we had a word with the accused man himself."

3

A short drive brought us to Chelsea Police Station where Jamison ushered us through into a small, bare room with white-washed walls which contained nothing but a desk, a mahogany filing cabinet and a few chairs. I was prepared for a change in my friend when he was shown into my presence but never had I seen such a transformation in a man. I had not seen him in the flesh for some years, it was true, but the photographs in newspapers and magazines of the tall, handsome, glossy-haired man had not prepared me for this pale, blanched creature with lacklustre eyes who was escorted into the office by two constables.

Tregorran was dressed only in a shirt and trousers and I noticed that he had no belt or braces, having to keep his hands on the latter garment to hold them up.

"Really, Inspector!" I protested. "He is not a common criminal!"

Jamison shot me a reproachful glance.

"It is necessary for his own good, Dr. Parker. We were afraid he might hang himself overnight. And I am afraid that whether he is your friend or no, he is a common criminal now."

I bit my lip and hurried over to the desk where Tregorran sat slumped, his dead, soulless eyes fixed on vacancy.

"I am sorry to see you like this," I mumbled, hardly knowing what I was saying.

The eyes painfully focused and at last I saw recognition in them. A shudder shook his frame.

"Ah, Parker! It was good of you to come. I am afraid you find me much changed."

I clasped the feeble hand held out to me and sat down at his side, conscious that Solar Pons and the Inspector had silently taken seats at the other side of the desk. I looked across at Jamison.

"He has been medically examined?"

"Of course, doctor. Our man found him incoherent and wandering in his mind. He is confused about yesterday's events, though that is natural enough."

Jamison drew his lips into a thin, straight line.

"He is sane enough to stand trial if that is what you were thinking," he said grimly.

Solar Pons leaned forward at the table and tented his thin fingers before him.

"We shall see, Jamison," he said crisply.

He fixed Tregorran with his penetrating eyes.

"Just tell us what happened yesterday in your own words and be as accurate and precise as possible as to detail."

Tregorran shook his head with a wan smile.

"That is just it, Mr. Pons. My mind is an absolutely confused blank. When the police told me I was accused of murdering Sylvia it was not only an appalling shock but a patent absurdity."

"Why do you say that, Mr. Tregorran?"

"Because it is the Gospel truth, Mr. Pons. My wife and I, after a period of great turbulence, were on quite amiable terms again. We were not living together, it is true; we both led separate lives and had done so for some time. But to say that I murdered her or that I even wanted to murder her is ridiculous!"

"Even in view of Miss Celia Thornton?" Jamison put in waspishly.

Tregorran turned white.

"You have seen her?"

Jamison nodded.

"We interviewed her last night. She did not deny that you had been intimate friends for some time."

Solar Pons turned to the Inspector,

"Who is this lady, Jamison?"

The Inspector had a mocking expression in his eyes.

"No doubt Mr. Tregorran can answer that, Mr. Pons."

Tregorran had a defiant expression on his face now.

"It was no secret that my wife and I were at daggers drawn, Mr. Pons. Celia and I had been lovers for a long time to be quite frank, Inspector."

"An excellent motive for murdering your wife, I should think," put in Jamison drily.

Tregorran shook his head wearily.

"Unfortunately, Celia and I had become estranged of late, also. It is a long story, gentlemen, and I will not bore you with it today. You were asking about yesterday, Mr. Pons?"

My companion inclined his head, his eyes never leaving Tregorran's face.

"Your day, hour by hour, Mr. Tregorran, if you please."

"It is very simply told, Mr. Pons. I rose at six a.m. to catch the light for a particular commission I am working on. I breakfasted at seven and by half-past I was already at work in my studio. I took a break for a cup of coffee at about ten-thirty a.m., and my wife arrived around eleven o'clock for work on her portrait."

"Tell me about that, Mr. Tregorran."

The haggard man at the table expressed surprise.

"There is nothing to tell, Mr. Pons."

Then his face cleared.

"You mean why did I wish to paint Sylvia's portrait after we had been on such bad terms? It was her request. Though she put it tactfully, I gathered that the commission came from an admirer. I am quite a good painter, you know, and there was nothing unusual in such an undertaking, even given the circumstances of our stormy marriage."

Solar Pons nodded.

"Quite so."

Tregorran passed a shaking hand over his forehead. He looked a hopeless figure slumped before us and I could not repress a twinge of pity.

"Mrs. Mandeville brought me my cup of coffee . . . "

Pons drew his eyebrows together in a frown of concentration. He glanced at Jamison.

"She did not mention that."

Tregorran shrugged.

"Probably an oversight, Mr. Pons. I did not see her. She merely rapped on the door and left the cup on the table outside. I left the cup there afterwards and it was presumably cleared away at lunch-time."

"I see. What happened when your wife arrived?"

"We chatted on perfunctory matters. Then I carried on with the sitting. Mrs. Mandeville brought my lunch at about twelve o'clock. I was concentrating on the painting and did not collect the tray until about twenty-past. Fortunately, Mrs. Mandeville had put up beer and sandwiches on this occasion or the food would have been cold."

"I see."

Solar Pons' eyes were very bright and piercing as he stared at the painter.

"Mrs. Tregorran ate nothing, I understand?"

The painter shook his head.

"I had asked for nothing for her as she always ate much later. Usually around two o'clock. That is much too late for me and I feel starved if I go beyond half-past twelve."

"Hmm."

Solar Pons sat staring silently at the wretched figure of the stricken painter.

"After your lunch, what then?"

"I continued painting, Mr. Pons. Everything was normal and from time to time I sipped at my glass of beer. Sylvia had gone out of her way to be pleasant and the thought of doing any harm to her was farthest from my mind. At about a quarter to two I felt faint."

"How did you know it was a quarter to two?"

Solar Pons leaned forward as though the answer had tremendous import.

"I heard the quarter hour strike from the cupola of a neighbouring church, Mr. Pons. Then I came over very faint. I must have lost consciousness because when I came to myself Relph and my gardener had battered down the door. I was incoherent and not making any sense, I am told. It was not until I found myself at Chelsea Police Station late that evening that I came fully to myself and realised that Sylvia was dead and that I was being charged with murder. For God's sake, help me, Mr. Pons!"

There was such abject misery in the words that, despite my old friend's obvious guilt, I felt a stab of pity for him. I looked at Pons and was astonished to see that he was smiling. However, he turned to me and said somewhat mockingly, "I begin to see light, Parker. We may yet make something of this."

Jamison gave a short laugh.

"Indeed, Mr. Pons. I had heard you were a magician but you will need to be a miracle worker to get Mr. Tregorran out of this."

I looked at my companion ruefully.

"I am afraid he is right, Pons."

"We shall see, Parker, we shall see," he returned equably and went on puffing at his pipe.

4

Miss Celia Thornton's residence was a large, white house approached by a circular carriage drive, in St. John's Wood. Our cab deposited us at the foot of a broad flight of steps and after a housekeeper had answered my companion's discreet ring at the bell, Pons had his card sent in. The woman returned almost immediately, an enigmatic expression on her bland, genteel face.

"Miss Celia is not here, Mr. Pons, but Miss Annabel will see you."

The woman who rose to greet us in the gracious sitting-room on the ground floor was of striking beauty. She advanced hesitantly, looking from one to the other of us.

"Mr. Pons?"

"This is he," I said, indicating my companion. "Lyndon Parker at your service."

"Sit down, gentlemen."

The brown eyes were shrewd beneath the masses of lustrous dark hair.

"Annabel Bolton. Celia and I share this house, as you probably know."

Pons' sharp eyes never left her face.

"No, I did not know, Miss Bolton. I expect you have guessed what brings me here?"

A cloud crossed the handsome features as Miss Bolton resumed her seat. She bit her lip.

"This wretched business of the painter Tregorran, Mr. Pons! A dreadful affair. Celia is well out of it."

"Out of her entanglement with Tregorran, Miss Bolton?"

The brown eyes flashed.

"Not only that, Mr. Pons! Celia has her own career to consider."

Solar Pons bit reflectively on the stem of the empty pipe he had produced from his pocket.

"Her own career, Miss Bolton?"

"Come, Mr. Pons. You surely cannot be unaware of Celia's brilliant and original contributions to scientific research?"

Pons stared at our fair companion as though thunderstruck.

"Miss Thornton. Of course! The experimental chemist whose researches into the nature of crystalline structures has advanced our knowledge so much. Pray forgive me. I did not connect the name at first with that of Mr. Tregorran's friend."

A faint flush suffused the cheeks of Miss Bolton.

"Former friend, Mr. Pons," she corrected my companion firmly.

Solar Pons put his pipe back into his pocket and sat bolt upright in his seat.

"That puts a different complexion on matters, Parker," he said softly. "Where could I find Miss Thornton?"

The young lady looked surprised.

"Why at her laboratory, of course, at this time of day. Though whether your visit will be welcome is another matter."

"We must risk that," said Solar Pons calmly. "But another occasion will do if today is not convenient."

Miss Bolton nodded, mentioning the research laboratory of a famous London hospital. Pons thanked her, noting the details in a small black notebook he sometimes used for such purposes.

"You may tell the lady we have called," he said, looking round the room, noting the text books that took up a great many of the shelves. "How remiss of me. I would take it as a favour if you would not mention my *faux pas* to your companion."

Annabel Bolton gave Pons a slight bow and included me in the smile which lurked behind her eyes.

"Certainly not, Mr. Pons. Good day."

No sooner were we outside the house than Pons uttered an exclamation and snapped his fingers in annoyance.

"Come, Parker!" he said urgently, guiding me down the pavement. "We must find a cab. There is not a moment to lose or vital evidence may be missing!"

"I am sure I do not know what you mean, Pons!" I said in amazement.

"I have been blind, Parker," said my companion as a cab turned the end of the crescent and pulled up obediently in response to his signal.

"We must get back to Chelsea at once."

"You are not going to see Miss Thornton, then?"

"Tut, Parker, that is quite unnecessary for the moment. Though I had arrived at certain theories the matter now becomes blindingly simple."

"I am glad you think so, Pons," I retorted with some asperity.

Solar Pons' deep-set eyes were fixed somewhere on a corner of the cab roof and it was obvious that his thoughts were far away.

"It is now just a question of deciding how the facts fit these new circumstances. We shall see, we shall see."

Back at Tregorran's residence Relph showed us quickly to the studio and then withdrew. Constable Mecker had just come on duty again and looked as surprised to see us as I felt. But he showed us in with a welcoming smile.

"I did not expect to see you back, Mr. Pons, but you are most welcome, gentlemen."

Solar Pons nodded sympathetically, his sharp eyes darting about the studio.

"You are finding it dull, of course?"

"The time does drag, sir. But I suppose one must get used to that in police routine."

"Indeed," I rejoined. "I have had many a long and boring vigil with Mr. Pons here in the course of some of his cases."

"Thank you, Parker," said Solar Pons crisply, but the little lights dancing in his eyes showed that he had not taken offence at my somewhat crass remark.

Pons moved over to Tregorran's easel, his casual manner belied by the sharpness of his eyes. He looked at the debris of the unfortunate artist's lunch which still stood by its side.

"Special export lager, with a gold foil seal, Parker. An expensive brand, too. That has great significance."

"I fail to see it, Pons."

"That is because your efforts are diverted in another direction altogether, Parker. Let us just consider the texture of this sandwich."

To my astonishment he picked up the crust of the sandwich left on the plate. The exclamation he made as he suddenly hurried toward the door almost startled me. I followed him down the corridor toward the glassed-in porch.

"The dust, Parker," he muttered. "It told a plain, unmistakable story, yet I did not read it aright. There are two impressions; one of Mrs. Mandeville's tray and the other of a single beer bottle and tumbler."

"I cannot..." I began when Pons rudely interrupted me and opened the inner porch door. He stood in silence for a moment looking at a large ceramic jar that stood midway between the two doors. It was obviously used as an umbrella stand because two sticks, one with a silver handle, were thrust into it. Pons' aquiline nostrils were quivering.

"Do you not smell it, Parker?"

Then I caught the same odour, an unpleasant, stale smell as of greasy food. Pons peered into the depths of the jar and gave a sharp exclamation of satisfaction.

"What do you make of that, Parker?"

I peered in over his shoulder.

"Good heavens, Pons! A plate of cold soup and something that looks like blackberry tart with cream."

Solar Pons smiled dreamily.

"Apple tart, I think you will find, Parker. Mr. Tregorran's lunch, undoubtedly."

He turned back to the inner door and examined it carefully.

"There is a keyhole here, partly concealed by the scrollwork.

That almost completes my case, I think. No, Parker, I am not yet quite ready to divulge the details. For that you must wait until tomorrow evening."

He led the way back into the house and downstairs at a trot so rapid that it left me breathless. Mrs. Mandeville, who was up to her elbows in flour in the kitchen, shared my surprise.

"Mr. Tregorran's lunch, Mrs. Mandeville," rapped Pons. "I omitted to ask you yesterday. It is of the utmost importance. What did you serve him?"

The housekeeper dried her hands on a cloth.

"Onion soup, his favourite, Mr. Pons. A bottle of his special export lager. And apple tart with cream. I like Mr. Tregorran to eat properly, though he often makes do with sandwiches if I am not careful."

"Thank you, Mrs. Mandeville," said Pons quietly. "I have one more piece to fit in the jigsaw but I think you have solved the problem for me. Come, Parker. I must crave Jamison's indulgence in the matter of the police laboratory and then write a letter. In the meantime I am afraid you must contain your impatience as best you can."

5

It was almost seven o'clock when I arrived at our cosy sitting-room at 7B Praed Street the following evening. I had a somewhat complicated case in the suburbs and had dined at a restaurant in Wimbledon on my way back. Pons had been enigmatic in the extreme all the previous evening and today had been absent on some mysterious errand in the morning. But when I saw him at lunch-time he had a sparkle and suppressed excitement in his manner. He rubbed his thin hands together and shuffled some official-looking documents so persistently that I twice had to ask him, at the lunch-table, to desist.

Afterward he wrote a message which he sealed in a plain envelope, addressed it to a destination he did not disclose and despatched it by special messenger. He chuckled as he sat by the fire, his spare form bathed in misty sunshine which straggled through from the street outside.

"If that does not bring our quarry to the net nothing will, Parker!"

"I am completely in the dark, Pons," I said, somewhat bitter-ly.

My friend laid a soothing hand on my arm.

"The philosophers counsel patience, Parker. In the mind that is once truly disciplined, as the good Marcus Aurelius has it. In a few hours you shall know everything that I myself know about this matter. When do you expect to return this evening?"

"At about seven, Pons."

My companion nodded.

"Excellent. I have arranged the appointment for eight o'clock. You should be in good time for the drama."

Now, as I entered the sitting-room, I was surprised to see that it was dark and completely empty. I switched on the light and was puzzled to hear a somewhat furtive step that seemed to come from my bedroom. I had not gone half a dozen paces across the room when Pons himself entered from his own room, blinking about him in the strong light.

"Apologies, my dear fellow. I felt rather tired after tea and have been catching up on my arrears of sleep."

I looked at him sharply. Such a situation was most unusual for Pons but he did yawn once or twice and his hair was

109

rumpled so I assumed that he had been lying down fully clothed in the dusk of his bedroom.

He looked alert enough now and bustled about, pulling up a third chair toward the table and looking sharply at the clock. He stopped in front of a mirror and put a careless hand up to smooth his hair.

"Now, Parker, we have only to possess ourselves in patience and with a little luck your friend Tregorran may cheat the hangman yet."

I stared at Pons in undisguised amazement.

"I have seen you do some remarkable things, Pons, but we know from the evidence and from the witnesses that there can be no doubt that Aramis Tregorran strangled his own wife."

"There is no doubt about it, Parker," said Pons calmly. "Yet in my opinion he is entirely innocent."

My jaw dropped and I gazed at my companion with mingled admiration and irritation. He saw the look in my eyes and his own danced with undisguised pleasure. He put a finger to his lips to enjoin caution and opened his tobacco pouch. In a few minutes he was completely surrounded by a cloud of aromatic blue smoke and he stayed like that, in complete silence, while I read *The Lancet* by the fire, for almost half an hour.

Our idyll was interrupted by a ring at the doorbell and then we heard an altercation in the hallway below; an excited female voice was opposed in a duet with the more placid tones of Mrs. Johnson. There followed scrambling footsteps on the stairs, our door was flung open unceremoniously and a panting, wild-eyed woman stood there, her black eyes flashing with anger and outrage as she stared first at me and then at my companion.

"Mr. Pons! Mr. Solar Pons! How dare you send me such a message! You have quite upset my work at the laboratory."

Solar Pons rose from his chair with a smile.

"The truth often does strike like a blow, Miss Thornton. Will you not close the door and sit down? You will find a comfortable chair yonder."

The imperious, dark-haired woman slammed the door back in its frame with a crash that seemed to shake the building. She stamped her foot as she stared at Pons.

"I will know what this outrageous note means before I leave this house!"

She flung a sheet of paper toward him and it came to rest near the foot of my chair. Solar Pons smiled thinly.

"You would do well to sit, Miss Thornton. I really do advise it. And Dr. Parker here, as a medical man, would prescribe the relaxed position as a tonic for the nerves."

The angry woman paused and made an impatient movement with her hand as though she would have flung something at my companion. Then she apparently thought better of it and sank sullenly into the chair indicated. I had picked up the paper and held it out to Pons. He merely gestured to me to read it.

It said:

Dear Miss Thornton,

If you wish to tell me all the facts about the murder of Mrs. Tregorran I shall be at my quarters at 7B Praed Street at eight o'clock this evening. I am in possession of the true circumstances and if you do not answer my summons you will have to deal directly with the official police.

Truly yours,
Solar Pons.

I put the sheet down on our table and looked across at the white, compressed face of Celia Thornton. She was a little more composed now.

"I am waiting, Mr. Pons," she said grimly.

"I shall not keep you, Miss Thornton, and will come directly to the point. We have heard from Mr. Tregorran that you and he had been intimate for some while, but that he had become reconciled with his wife. Jealousy is a great distorter of human relations."

The woman opposite us had a strange smile on her taut features.

"I have not denied my relationship with Tregorran," she said. "I gave a statement to the police yesterday."

"I am well aware of that, Miss Thornton. What I am saying here today is that you know a great deal more than you have stated about Mrs. Tregorran's death and the charge of murder that is now hanging over her husband."

Celia Thornton tossed her head and looked from Pons to me and then back to my companion again.

"The implication is preposterous, Mr. Pons. You will have to do better than that."

"I intend to," said Solar Pons calmly. "Let us just recall the sequence of events. Mrs. Tregorran is found strangled in a locked studio, her husband nearby, incoherent and unaware of what has happened. I questioned the unfortunate man yesterday and I am convinced that he is speaking the truth. What we are left with is something more complicated."

Celia Thornton sat watching Solar Pons with glittering eyes but said nothing.

"The first thing that struck me about the case was a locked door without a key," Pons went on. "That was extremely significant and I commended it to you, Parker. I will now suggest the possible sequence of events and Miss Thornton will no doubt correct me if I am wrong. Tregorran had an unhappy marriage and had formed an association with you. But when he said that he was becoming reconciled to his wife, you became extremely jealous and there were violent quarrels. We have that from Tregorran himself. You concocted an elaborate scheme for revenge that would punish both the wife whom you hated and your lover also."

"Prove it!" Miss Thornton snapped.

"I am endeavouring so to do," said Solar Pons equably. "Your love had turned to hate and you would stop at nothing to strike back at your former lover and the obstacle to your happiness. In your liaison with Tregorran you had obviously visited his studio. He has not told me so but I infer it as it is central to my theory."

"I knew the studio," the woman said with a curious smile. "The fact is not in question and easy enough to check. I admit it."

Solar Pons inclined his head gravely.

"Very well, then. You knew the studio and the layout of the house. You had your own keys to the doors. On the day of the murder you went to the house and entered by the archway unseen. It is easy enough to do. Instead, however, of entering the studio by the staircase entrance, you opened the inner door to the corridor, of which you retained a key. You stationed yourself in the angle of the corridor and waited until Relph brought Tregorran's lunch-tray.

"When he had tapped on the door and withdrawn you quickly went to the table, removed the plate of soup and the dessert. To do that—and you thought you had not very much time—you removed the bottle of lager and put it down on the table. I know that because I have seen the marks in the dust and it puzzled me at first why this should be so. The explanation then became clear to me. You put the food within the large vase used as an umbrella stand in the annexe."

Celia Thornton's eyes were very bright.

"Preposterous! Why should I wish to do that?"

Solar Pons held up his hand.

"I am just coming to that. You returned to the table and put the beer bottle and tumbler back on the tray. Beside it you placed your specially prepared sandwich."

It was very quiet in the room now and I looked at Pons, my puzzlement evident on my features.

"You then resumed your vigil at the end of the corridor. When Tregorran had taken the lunch-tray back into the studio, which was not for some time, you crept back down the corridor. You quietly locked the door and took the key away."

"Why was that, Pons?"

"Because, Parker, there had to be time for Miss Thornton's plan to work and she did not want the sitting interrupted. It was also vital for the scheme's success that Tregorran should be seen by witnesses to be sane and in possession of himself."

"I am afraid I do not see . . . "

"Tut, Parker, Miss Thornton herself will give us the ingenious explanation in a moment or two."

Our visitor drew herself up, little spots of red blazing on her cheeks.

"I find your questions offensive, your implications odious and your conclusions entirely erroneous, Mr. Pons."

Solar Pons drew reflectively on his pipe, little stipples of fire making patterns on his thin, ascetic features.

"Indeed. You face it out well enough, Miss Thornton, but you know in your heart that your cruel and ingenious scheme has been discovered. Let us just take things a step further. When I first visited the studio I did not, of course, know of your possible involvement in the matter. When I learned that you were a brilliant experimental chemist things began to fall into place."

"I see, Pons," I began, light dawning in dark places.

"No doubt, Parker," said Solar Pons crisply.

"I had noted that the lager was a special export brand, sealed with foil and a metal cap. That indicated to me that it was unlikely anything could have been introduced into the beer. But it could have acted as a catalyst for something else that should not have been in the food. Where I made my big mistake was in not detecting the substitution earlier. I had asked Mrs. Mandeville and Relph about Tregorran's lunch but none of us had thought to mention its composition. And then there was the matter of the missing key. You showed considerable courage in that respect, as indeed, throughout this dreadful business."

Solar Pons paused as though expecting a reply from Celia Thornton but she remained silent, staring at him with a tight, set face.

"To avoid any suspicion over the locked door, you came back to the studio at dead of night, let yourself in by the back entrance and replaced the key in the door. Either the constable on duty was asleep or had his back turned. It took tremendous nerve but now that I have met you I have no doubt that you would have managed it. And indeed, you would have to have done so, as the key was incontrovertibly back in the door when I examined it, though police and other witnesses had said it was nowhere to be found. It was unfortunate for you that its loss had already been noted."

"I follow you, Pons," I said admiringly.

"A little late, Parker, but I did commend the fact to you," Pons continued.

"If I were to save my client's life there was only one possibility remaining. It was contained in the section of sandwich which fortunately remained unconsumed. I went back to the studio and abstracted it. The police laboratory analysis yielded some interesting information. I have their report here."

Solar Pons smiled thinly and produced some sheets of paper from his pocket.

"But you, as an outstanding chemist, would already know its contents, would you not? Be so good as to glance over this, Parker."

I read the documents with increasing admiration.

"I see, Pons!" I cried excitedly. "Ergot! Of course. The sandwich had been made of rye diseased with ergot."

"Correct," said Pons, biting on the stem of his pipe. "It was an extremely clever and utterly diabolical plot that only a scientist's mind like Miss Thornton's would be capable of conceiving as an instrument of revenge. Bread made with rye diseased with ergotism would affect the victim in what way, Parker?"

"Why, he would very probably go mad, Pons!" I exclaimed. "Ergot produces lysergic acid and in the form of lysergic acid diethylamide would induce a schizophrenic condition."

"Exactly, Parker. As soon as I got this report I studied the literature on the subject. There was a village in France where the local baker produced a batch of bread from diseased rye some years ago. The entire village went mad. There were several deaths, including one where a husband stabbed his wife and a number of people launched themselves from tree-tops in the erroneous belief that they could fly. I have no doubt Miss Thornton is extremely familiar with the literature."

Solar Pons fixed grim, accusing eyes on Celia Thornton who sank back in her chair.

"A wicked, diabolical plot," he repeated. "Such as could only emanate from the brain of a revenge-crazed woman who was also a very talented scientist."

Celia Thornton half-rose from her chair.

"Prove it!" she said defiantly.

"I have already done so," said Solar Pons.

"It is all hearsay!" the woman said wildly. "You have not a scrap of evidence. There is nothing to connect me with having been in the studio."

Solar Pons shook his head, drawing something from his pocket.

"I am sorry to contradict a lady but this object irrefutably places you at the scene of the crime."

He produced a small crimson leather purse which bore the gold monogram C.T.

"Your initials, I believe? I found this beneath the table in the hall of Tregorran's house!"

The woman sprang to her feet, a shocking transformation in her face.

"You are right, Mr. Pons. I did all those things you said. But you will have a hard time proving it, let alone bringing me to court. Where is your evidence? We three are alone within these walls. You have taken no notes of our conversation. It will be my word against yours. The whole thing is preposterous."

To my astonishment Solar Pons was smiling.

"I only wanted to hear it from your own lips, Miss Thornton. You have confirmed all my suppositions. As for the purse, you may put your mind at rest. You did not drop it at the scene of the crime. I took it from the hall of your residence yesterday when Dr. Parker and I called on your friend, Miss Annabel Bolton! But it was enough to elicit a confession from you for my purposes."

He turned to me.

"It is true that Miss Thornton could not know exactly what would happen in that studio. But the end was tragedy and in one blow she would have removed both her rival and her lover if I had not finally put two and two together."

"You have done brilliantly, Pons, as always."

Solar Pons waved away my congratulations.

"Even so, it was an erratic form of revenge, though she might well have driven Tregorran permanently mad. I am told the eating of such diseased material can take that form."

"That is why she locked the door," I said. "In Tregorran's case it took only two hours for the ergot to have that sensational effect. Enhanced, of course by the beer he had drunk, which sent the poison more quickly round his system. In some people it might have taken a deal longer."

Celia Thornton stood facing us with twitching features. She fought to retain control.

"You are very clever, Mr. Pons. Everything you have said is true. But as I have already stated, you will never bring me to trial or clear Tregorran. It is too late for that."

"I think not," said Solar Pons calmly. "You may come in, Inspector Jamison. Ah, there you are, Mecker! I trust you took an accurate note of Miss Thornton's statement?"

Celia Thornton fell back against the table with a cry of

anguish and I started up in astonishment as the forms of Inspector Jamison and the constable emerged from the shadowy doorway of Pons' bedroom. I stared at my companion, stupefied.

"We have the statement, Mr. Pons. Celia Thornton, I charge you with complicity in the murder of Sylvia Tregorran by administering a dangerous drug and warn you that anything you say may be taken down and used in evidence."

The girl stared round at us wildly and then collapsed into her chair in a storm of sobbing.

Jamison nodded to Mecker.

"Best take her down to the station," he said awkwardly. "We'll sort out everything there."

When the constable had departed with his distraught charge, Jamison sat down in the vacated place and looked at my companion with grudging admiration.

"Well, Mr. Pons, you have done it again. I take off my hat to you."

"Praise indeed, Inspector," said Solar Pons drily.

"Though how we're to get through the legal and other tangles I don't know," Jamison continued.

He scratched his head.

"The main thing is that we have saved an innocent man from the rope," said Pons. "The rest is for the courts to unravel."

Jamison sighed heavily.

"When clever people go wrong there is the devil to pay," he observed sagely.

Solar Pons passed over Celia Thornton's purse to him.

"You had better take that, Jamison. My methods were a little unfair but we are dealing with a cruel and implacable woman."

I looked at the open door of Pons' bedroom.

"So that was why you were so furtive when I came back," I said somewhat bitterly.

Solar Pons smiled and laid his hand on my arm.

"I am afraid I could not let you into our little secret, my dear fellow. It was imperative to get that confession down on paper through the official police. Your feelings are so honestly transparent that you could not have kept up the masquerade." He blew a cloud of smoke thoughtfully from his pipe. "Let us hope it will have taught Mr. Tregorran a much-needed lesson. Between the two of them he was bound to come to destruction sooner or later."

Murder at the Zoo

1

"GOOD EVENING, PARKER!"

"Good evening, Pons!"

Solar Pons shook the droplets of water from his great-coat and stamped his feet; his lean, feral face wearing a humorous expression. It was a foul, foggy evening in late November, and to make matters worse the capital was shrouded in a weeping rain that seemed to penetrate to one's very bones with its coldness. I had spent a frustrating day on my round of patients and had been very glad to come in at six o'-clock and take refuge in our comfortable quarters at 7B Praed Street.

It was now turned seven and I was pleased to see Pons for I knew that Mrs. Johnson, our amiable landlady, was delaying our evening meal until his arrival. I had not missed the ironic tone in Pons' voice with its implied commentary on the day and the subtle reference to the pending meal and now I vacated my comfortable chair and came forward to help my friend out of his soaked hat and coat.

"Thank you, Parker. As usual, you are a model of thoughtfulness and consideration."

"Good of you to say so, Pons. You won't mind me mentioning it, but you look as though you had just come out of a particularly muddy section of the line on the Ypres Salient."

Solar Pons laughed, drawing close to the fire and watching the steam ascend from the toe-caps of his stout boots.

"You are not so far short of the truth, Parker. I have been down to Hoxton ferreting about on the site of a new housing estate. The swindles of Jabez Wilson are about to be put a term to. The mud and debris on the site was somewhat reminiscent of the late war, I must say. If you will just give me a few minutes to change my suit and clean up a little, Mrs. Johnson may serve as soon as she likes."

"Excellent, Pons."

I went down to acquaint Mrs. Johnson with the gist of Pons' message and when I returned, my companion was restored to his immaculate self. He sat in his favourite armchair, his lean fingers tented before him, and stared reflectively at the dancing firelight in the grate.

"Might there be some notes for me in this business, Pons?" I asked.

My companion smiled.

"I fear not, Parker. It is too mundane for your chronicles and though 'The Adventure of the Hoxton Builder' might raise considerable expectation in the reader, I fear it would fall far short of your best efforts in the field. Though Scotland Yard will be glad to learn that Mr. Wilson is in the net."

We were interrupted at that moment by the entry of our landlady with a large tray containing a wide assortment of steaming dish-covers, from which came a variety of enticing aromas. We did full justice to our supper and when we had pushed back our plates and poured the coffee I was beginning to take a more sanguine view of the world.

Solar Pons, his empty pipe in his mouth, was absorbed in the evening paper and there was an agreeable silence between us for half an hour. Eventually he threw down the newspaper with an exclamation of disgust.

"This zoo business is intriguing, Parker, but the press has got hold of the wrong end of the stick."

"I have not seen it, Pons."

"The item is there, my dear fellow. It has been running for some weeks. I am convinced there is more to it than meets the eye. But you know the penchant the yellow press has for distortion and sensationalism."

"Come, Pons," I said, laughing. "You will be guilty of the very same fault of which you accuse your clients. I do not know the first thing about the matter."

Solar Pons smiled thinly and stroked his chin in a manner which had long become familiar to me.

"I apologise unreservedly, Parker. I always keep abreast of the criminal news and I must confess I sometimes forget that others do not always share my somewhat esoteric interests. You will find most of the salient features in this evening's journal, though pathetically tuppence coloured."

There was indeed a huge heading I saw, as I picked up the newspaper which Pons had laid down. The article was blazoned: GROTESQUE MYSTERY AT ZOO. IS THERE A PHANTOM AT WORK?

I read it with increasing interest. The gist of it was as follows. It appeared that a mysterious night-time intruder at the Zoological Gardens at Regents Park had been leaving a trail of havoc behind him. The events had begun in October when a nocturnal prowler had opened monkey cages and chimpanzees and monkeys had run riot throughout the night. An incident the following week was more serious, when a Bengal tigress had been loosed from the Lion House:

What might have been tragedy for the keepers when they first came on duty in the early morning, was narrowly averted when the Head Keeper, Norman Stebbins, an exceptionally strong man, came to the aid of his colleague. He held the main doors by sheer strength until help was summoned. The beast was eventually netted and recaptured.

"A fine effort, Pons," I commented about Stebbins' feat. "Putting his arm through in place of the door-bar like that."

"Indeed, Parker. Another case of nature imitating art."

"I do not follow, Pons."

"Mr. Stebbins would appear to have followed the example set by Kate Barlass, Parker."

My companion laughed at the blank incomprehension on my face.

"No matter, Parker. Pray continue."

I read on with mounting bewilderment. The events certainly seemed weird and disconnected. Other animals had been let loose, including ostriches and, in one case, a rhinoceros. Damage to property and danger to life had been the principal features here though only one man, an under-keeper named Billings, had been slightly injured.

"The people at the Zoo have been extremely lucky, Pons," I commented, folding the paper.

"Have they not, Parker. What do you make of it?"

"I have not yet finished the item, Pons, but there seems little point in any of it, unless some member of the public has a grudge against the Zoo authorities."

"That is a possibility we must not overlook."

I looked at my companion sharply.

"You talk as though you expect to be retained in the matter, Pons."

"I must confess I am inordinately interested."

I read on in silence for another minute or so.

"This business of the spiders in the tropical house, Pons, is loathsome in the extreme. The Head Keeper had another narrow escape there."

"Did he not?"

"It is bizarre and inexplicable, Pons. I see that there is no evidence that any of the entrances or gates to the Zoological Gardens have been tampered with. Though the person who entered the Tropical House broke a glass door in order to do so, before letting those dreadful creatures escape. And locks on cages were smashed."

Solar Pons rubbed his thin hands together and picked up his coffee cup with an expression of enthusiasm dancing in his eyes.

"The police are completely baffled, Pons."

"I am not surprised to hear you say so."

"It says here," I went on, reading from the newspaper. "public alarm is growing and the activities of what has come to be called The Phantom of the Zoo are becoming more bold and daring. Already life has been endangered and it is only a question of time before a fatality occurs. The cunningness of the Phantom ... "

"Pschaw, Parker," said Solar Pons, interrupting me rudely.

"Pray spare me the rubbishy fulminations of the popular press. This is all very well for the romantic shop girl or the more lurid manifestations of the cinema, but we continue to apply the ratiocinative processes at 7B. As I have observed before, this agency stands foursquare upon the ground."

"That is all very well, Pons," said I, refolding the paper and passing it back to him. "You have often remarked to me that such remarkable mysteries cannot be solved at long distance. And if you have not been retained, I do not see..."

"There is no mystery to be solved," said Solar Pons calmly. "Or, to be more precise, we can discount these rubbishy stories of Phantoms and prowlers of the night. A human hand is at work here, opening cages, throwing back bolts, breaking windows. That goes without saying. The method of entry to the Gardens is a little more interesting but not difficult for the right person. It is the motive which interests me. Human nature is one of the most fascinating of studies, Parker. I commend it to you."

"I am not entirely insulated from human nature in my profession, Pons," I commented somewhat stiffly.

Solar Pons smiled wryly.

"*Touché*, Parker. It was not my intention to give offence. But you have not yet looked at the 'Stop Press'."

I again picked up the paper from the table and turned to the item at the bottom right-hand corner of the front page, which he had underlined.

I read:

EARLY ARREST EXPECTED. Scotland Yard announced tonight they expect early arrest of Phantom of the Zoo. See story Page 1.

"That would appear to be the end of the matter, Pons."

"We shall see, Parker, we shall see," said Pons, an enigmatic smile on his face.

As he spoke there came an imperative rapping at the front door, followed by an agitated ringing of the bell. A minute or two later Mrs. Johnson's well-scrubbed face, with its heavy coils of hair, appeared round the door.

"A young man to see you, Mr. Pons. He is in a dreadful state. He says it is about the Phantom of the Zoo."

2

Pons looked at me in silence for a moment, a slightly mocking expression in his eyes.

"Show him in, Mrs. Johnson," he said swiftly. "Pray do not go, Parker. I may have need of your commonsense and ready wit."

"You do me too much honour, Pons," I mumbled, slewing my chair round so that I could command a better view of the door.

A young man of about twenty-eight entered, with tousled fair curly hair. He was roughly-dressed in a dark blue uniform but there was an air of such honesty and decency about him, notwithstanding his haggard and distraught expression, that I warmed to him immediately. He looked from one to the other of us, then unerringly made for Solar Pons and held out his hand as though in mute appeal.

"Mr. Solar Pons? I am in most desperate trouble, sir. I do not know which way to turn."

Solar Pons looked at him with a reassuring expression.

"Do not disturb yourself, young man. Sit down there. No

doubt a cup of coffee would not come amiss on such a cold evening. If you would just do the honours, Mrs. Johnson."

Our landlady bustled about the table, making sure our guest was settled comfortably before she withdrew to the privacy of her own quarters. The young man was silent for a moment after she had quitted the room, his thick, spatulate fingers gripped convulsively round the cup as he took long, deep draughts of the black coffee.

"I do not seem to have caught your name," said my companion when our visitor seemed a little more himself.

"I am sorry, sir. This business has fair thrown me, Mr. Pons. And now that I am suspected, my life is not worth the living."

He gazed fiercely at us for a moment and then relaxed again.

"My name is John Hardcastle, gentlemen. I'm an under-keeper at the Lion House at the Zoological Gardens, where all these terrible things have been going on."

"Indeed," said Solar Pons, a twinkle in his eyes. "This is my friend and colleague, Dr. Lyndon Parker. I take it you have no objection to him hearing your little story?"

Our visitor shook his head.

"By no means. It takes some believing, sir, but I ask you to believe I am innocent."

"Come, Hardcastle," said Pons in a soothing voice. "Drink your coffee, have another and proceed with your story in a connected manner, if you please."

We both waited while Hardcastle poured himself more coffee with a hand that trembled slightly, despite himself.

"You've read the stories in the papers, Mr. Pons?"

"I am *au fait* with the salient points. Just exactly how you come to be connected with this affair is not quite clear at present. You are employed at the Zoo, as you have already told me. You are an old soldier; have seen much fighting in France where your health was broken; you have been wounded; and you are fond of pigeons; but these facts tell me little about your present problems."

Our visitor stared at Pons open-mouthed, his coffee cup half-raised from the saucer.

"Good heavens, Mr. Pons, the staff at the Zoo told me about you. They said you were some kind of magician, but I do not see how you could possibly know all these things."

"They are true, then?"

"Near enough, Mr. Pons. But how..."

"It was simple enough," said Solar Pons, giving me a mischievous little glance.

"You are a young man of some twenty-eight years, of vigorous aspect and in rude health, apart from your current agitation, yet your face is marked by illness. By your age it follows therefore that you would have served in the late conflict, as zoo-keeping was not a reserved occupation, to the best of my recollection."

"Correct, Mr. Pons."

"Yet I noticed as you came through the door that you had a slight limp in your left leg. It was the merest conjecture, but I immediately concluded that you had been wounded in the war. When I see a scrap of wound ribbon on your uniform jacket there, my conclusion is confirmed. When I see next to it the ribbon of the Mons Star, it is no great feat of reasoning to deduce that you were in the infantry and had seen heavy fighting."

"Again correct in every respect, Mr. Pons," said our visitor, awe and bewilderment on his frank, open face.

"I was a corporal in the Coldstreams. Lucky all through the

war but caught some shrapnel in the leg only three months from the armistice. I had trench-fever too and incipient tuber-culosis and was laid up for a long time after the war, though I am fit enough now."

"I am glad to hear it," I put in. "As a medical man, my diagnosis exactly."

"You are ever reliable, Parker," said Solar Pons gravely.

"But the pigeons, Pons?"

"Ah, that was the purest flight of fancy, Parker. Mr. Hardcastle has some cuts on his left hand. That may have something to do with his work in the Lion House, though I am sure he would not be careless enough to get within striking distance of his charges. But I noticed a series of minute red scratches on the first finger of his right hand. Only a pigeon-fancier gets those. The birds perch and alight on the right hand and sometimes their sharp claws may inflict tiny scratches. It would take a deal of time to collect such a finger as our young friend there."

"That is so, Mr. Pons," said Hardcastle.

"There is no tripping you, Pons," I complained bitterly.

Solar Pons laughed shortly.

"I am far from infallible, Parker. But we stray from the point."

"I am not a rich man, Mr. Pons," said our visitor anxiously. "I do not know what your fee would be..."

"Tut, man, let us not quibble about trifles," said Solar Pons impatiently. "You need not worry on that score. If a case interests me I sometimes remit my fee altogether. And this one promises a maximum of interest. Pray proceed without further delay."

Some of the colour was coming back to the young keeper's cheeks. He looked a fine, manly figure in his tight-fitting uniform as he sat opposite, twisting his peaked cap shyly in his strong, capable hands.

"They all think I'm guilty, Mr. Pons," he said quietly. "Even my girl, Alice. The only one who believes in me is the Head Keeper and the man in charge of the Lion House, Mr. Hodgson. He has been most helpful. You see, Mr. Pons, almost everyone at the Zoo thinks I did all these terrible things like letting Sheba out. Not to mention the damage."

He swallowed nervously. Then, encouraged by Pons' reassuring look, he went on.

"I love the work there, Mr. Pons. I wouldn't do anything to harm the Zoo, the animals or the visitors. Let alone my colleagues. But they found things in my locker. I don't know exactly what. Someone called the police, you see. I only heard about it in a roundabout way. My girl Alice came round early this morning to warn me. So I cut out. I wandered about all day. Then I remembered what I'd heard about you and decided to ask your help."

Solar Pons shook his head.

"Unwise, Hardcastle," he said gently. "It was the worst thing you could have done. If the police suspect you, as you suggest, and wish to interview you, they will find you soon enough."

There was dismay on the young man's face.

"I am sorry, Mr. Pons. I probably lost my head. I felt trapped, you see."

"I understand the feeling," I said sympathetically. "But Mr. Pons is right. We must go straight to the Zoo. We will both support you."

"Hold fast, Parker," said Pons with a light laugh. "I make allowances for your enthusiasm, my dear fellow, but this is my case and I dictate the conditions. I have not even agreed to take it as yet."

"I beg your pardon, Pons," I said apologetically. "I naturally assumed..."

Solar Pons held up his hand and Hardcastle, who had been rising to his feet, subsided gently in his chair.

"Do not concern yourselves. I have decided to take the case. Unless I am a worse judge of character than I imagine, Mr. Hardcastle is a transparently honest man. But I have not yet finished my questions."

He got up briskly.

"Now, Hardcastle, cast your mind back. I want to know more about these incidents; what your movements were; and particularly what things were found in your locker." He glanced at the clock in the corner. "There is nothing to be gained by a visit to the Zoo at this hour of the evening. The premises will be closed and the authorities will not welcome us. There will be time enough tomorrow. But a visit to the police is an entirely different matter. We must make contact with them tonight and have our story ready. Superintendent Heathfield, I think. Scotland Yard are already engaged in the matter." He turned back to me. "Now, Parker, I am sorry to turn you out again but I would be grateful if you would hail a cab. I will finish questioning Hardcastle here *en route* to the Yard."

☘ 3

When I returned to 7B Pons was already dressed for the street and our client was wearing a suit of gleaming oilskins which Mrs. Johnson had hung on a peg in the hall. Pons flung me a glance of approval.

"Hardcastle has just been telling me about the material discovered in his locker. An axe which had been used to smash a kiosk, fragments of wood still on it; some red paint similar to that which daubed a restaurant wall a few weeks ago; duplicate keys to some of the animal houses; a pair of gloves covered with paint-stains."

I stared at Pons sombrely.

"It looks bad on the face of it, Pons."

"Does it not, Parker. But there is a factor of great significance."

He smiled reassuringly at Hardcastle's doleful face as we descended the stairs to the lower hall.

"And what is that Pons?"

There is no key to Hardcastle's locker and in fact none of the lockers belonging to the staff of the Lion House are ever locked."

"I fail to see the importance, Pons."

Tut, Parker. Use your ratiocinative processes. If the locker had been secured things would have looked black. But in such a situation anyone could have placed the material there."

"I see, Pons. Of course."

Solar Pons stroked his ear with a thin finger.

"In fact, assuming Hardcastle's innocence, I have never heard of such a fatuous and clumsy attempt to implicate anyone. But it gives rise to some intriguing possibilities. There is a good deal more here than meets the eye. It is a pity you cannot remember more about the incriminating material in your locker, Hardcastle. I appreciate you heard most of the details from your young lady, but you should have paid closer attention."

"I am afraid I was too agitated at the time," said our client apologetically.

He led the way down the steps to where the taxi waited and a few moments later we were lurching through the fog and rain toward our destination. On arrival at Scotland Yard Solar Pons sent up his card and we were rapidly shown to a discreet room on the third floor where Superintendent Stanley Heathfield had his office. He himself rose from his desk as a plain-clothes officer showed us in, his eyes gleaming with pleasure.

"You know Dr. Parker, of course," said Solar Pons casually. "This young man is a client of mine. I will introduce him presently."

"As you wish, Mr. Pons."

Superintendent Heathfield waved us into comfortable chairs and went back to sit at his desk. A number of sporting prints in gilt frames were hung on the green-painted walls of his room and a gas fire burned comfortably in the grate.

"You are working late, Superintendent."

"You know very well this is our usual routine, Pons. Fencing for information, are you?"

Solar Pons leaned forward in his chair and smiled thinly.

"Just sounding out the ground, Superintendent."

"There is a great deal on, Mr. Pons. And I am expecting a visitor. But it must be something of great importance that brings you here on such a foul evening. Perhaps you are stuck on a little problem? Well, we are always happy to assist at the Yard."

Solar Pons smiled again.

"*Touché*, Superintendent. You are in fine form this evening, I see."

Heathfield's eyes twinkled as he glanced round at us in turn.

"Have some tea, gentlemen. I have just taken the liberty of ordering a tray."

He sat back at his desk and examined his perfectly manicured finger-nails as a woman in dark overalls entered and set out the cups and a pot on a corner of the desk. When we were alone again he was silent as he poured. Hardcastle rose clumsily and passed the cups to us. Heathfield sat back and regarded us with quizzical brown eyes. With his tall figure and clipped, iron-grey moustache, he looked more like a dapper Army officer than ever.

"We have not worked together since that business of Elihu Cook Stanmore, Mr. Pons."

"This is nothing like that, Superintendent. Just a little puzzle connected with London Zoo."

Superintendent Heathfield had straightened behind the desk now and his eyes were no longer humorous.

"Little puzzle or no, Mr. Pons, it is certainly no joke. I am having to deploy a great many people in order to catch this madman who is endangering life and limb."

Pons' eyes caught our client's and then swivelled to the Superintendent again.

"Something has happened today?"

Heathfield nodded.

"It was in the evening paper but you may have missed it. Someone let out a Polar bear. Nasty business. One attendant badly injured. I had to get some marksmen in and shoot the brute."

Hardcastle had turned white and his eyes held a mute appeal as he stared at Pons. My companion appeared oblivious to him, however, his eyes apparently fixed vacantly in space.

"Dear me, Superintendent. You have been on the spot?"

Heathfield shook his head.

"I have just returned from a murder investigation in Surrey, Mr. Pons. We are under some pressure at the moment. But I am on my way to the Zoo shortly, if you would care to accompany me. Sir Clive Mortimer, the President of the Zoological Society, is coming over. No doubt he is enraged and will be critical of police methods. It is to be expected. I think it only right to go and see for myself, though this confounded Phantom is proving incredibly elusive."

"Well, well," said Solar Pons in a monotone. "Perhaps you will have some news for him. I would like you to meet my client here. John Hardcastle is under-keeper at the Lion House and a young man who is unhappy about this whole affair."

There was a long moment of silence as the Superintendent stared at Pons. Hardcastle had gone white and sat as though rooted to his chair, beads of perspiration streaking his face. Heathfield half-rose and then seated himself again.

"I am glad that he has come in," he said mildly. "He has nothing to fear if he has a clear conscience."

"That is what I have told him," said Solar Pons. "Though I am glad to have it confirmed from your own lips."

Heathfield leaned forward and pressed a button on his desk. A door in the far corner of the room opened and a tall, frosty-haired man came in. He looked incuriously at the Superintendent.

"This is Detective-Inspector Glaister. I would like you to take a statement from Mr. Hardcastle here. He is the man we wish to question in connection with this business at the Zoological Gardens. He is the client of Mr. Solar Pons, whom I believe you know."

The Inspector smiled and came over to Pons and shook his hand cordially.

"Glad to see you again, Mr. Pons."

He waited while Hardcastle got to his feet. At a gesture from Pons Heathfield hesitated a moment and then added, "When you have finished with Mr. Hardcastle bring him over to the Zoo, will you. I shall be there with Mr. Pons and Dr. Parker."

"Very good, sir."

Our client went out apprehensively with the big officer. Heathfield put down his cup with a clink in the silence.

"If all is as you say, Mr. Pons, he has nothing to fear. Let us just hope he has been telling the truth."

"This business is all too curious to be the work of that young man, Superintendent," said Solar Pons.

Heathfield opened his mouth to answer but at that moment there came a deferential tap at the door and a uniformed Sergeant appeared to announce Sir Clive Mortimer. Pons and I would have withdrawn but Heathfield gestured to us to remain. The peppery little man who bounced into the room hesitated on seeing the three of us, but then squared his shoulders and advanced grimly toward the Superintendent's desk.

"I must say, Superintendent, that this is outrageous. Absolutely outrageous. That this scoundrel can lay waste to the Zoological Gardens in such a manner without being detected is quite beyond my comprehension."

Sir Clive spluttered as if he had run out of steam and glared at Heathfield belligerently. He had a pink face almost like a child's, with feathery white hair and a thin smear of moustache like lather. With his old-fashioned frock-coat, his dark raincoat and the black wideawake hat he carried in his hand, he resembled an illustration out of a nineteenth-century volume by Dickens or Wilkie Collins.

"Please compose yourself, Sir Clive. Have a cigar, sir. I assure you we are doing all we can. Allow me to present Mr. Solar Pons and his colleague Dr. Lyndon Parker."

The little man brightened.

"Mr. Pons. The eminent consulting detective?"

He came forward to shake hands with us both, then turned back to give a frosty glance to Heathfield.

"Is it too much to hope that Mr. Pons has been retained in this matter? I would give a great deal if it were so."

Inspector Heathfield chuckled with amusement.

"Mr. Pons is already connected with the affair, Sir Clive. One of your keepers, Hardcastle, has fallen under suspicion. Mr. Pons has been engaged to represent him."

"Hardcastle?"

The little man wrinkled up his face.

"Well, I know nothing of the details, Superintendent. But I am responsible to the Fellows and the Society's Council. We have never had anything like this in all our long history. I hope that it will shortly be cleared up."

He came close to my companion and peered sharply in his face.

"And I trust your man is innocent, Mr. Pons. Though I have no doubt you will shortly get to the bottom of the business. I have little faith in the London police."

Solar Pons smiled.

"You are too flattering in my case, Sir Clive. And too harsh in your strictures on the official force. I have no doubt that between us we shall introduce light into what has hitherto been murky."

"Well, you may well be right, Mr. Pons," said Sir Clive grudgingly. "Now, Superintendent, I believe you wish to see me privately. After that, I am at your service. I would like to return to the Gardens at once. Some of my colleagues are standing by at my office there."

"Certainly, Sir Clive. If you would come into this inner

room for a few minutes. I am sure you do not mind waiting a short while, Mr. Pons."

"By all means, Superintendent."

When we were alone Solar Pons stretched himself out on his chair, put his long legs in front of him and lit his pipe. He wreathed blue smoke at the ceiling. His eyes were twinkling.

"Well, Parker, what do you think of this business?"

"It would seem dark and impenetrable, Pons. Assuming that your client, Hardcastle, is innocent. Apart from everything else it is completely pointless."

"Is it not. Yet does not the sheer welter of events and the degree of mischief involved suggest something to you?"

I stared at my companion in astonishment.

"I do not follow you, Pons."

"It would not be the first time, Parker. Just use those faculties of intelligence that you so often bring to your medical diagnoses."

"Ah, well, Pons, that is a matter of science, whose limits are well sign-posted with text-book examples."

Solar Pons shot me a wry smile.

"But detection is an equally exact science, Parker. Every apparently disconnected fact has its place in the diagnosis. Just as you draw logical conclusions from your patient's perspiration, breathing and location of pain so do I similarly read a connected sequence of events from crushed blades of grass; cigarette ash carelessly scattered; or the angle of a wine-glass. Let me just have your thoughts on the present troubles at Regent's Park Zoo."

"You are right, Pons, of course," I replied. "But I fear I make a poor diagnostician in your sphere of life. Each to his own profession."

"Tut, Parker, you do yourself poor justice. You are constantly improving in your reading of events. For example, what motive would the person or persons committing malicious damage bring to these senseless acts?"

Pons stared at me through the wreathing blue coils of smoke from his pipe.

"It is just in those areas that I am such a poor reasoner, Pons."

"Pschaw, the matter is so simple as to be obvious. I have already given you the clue in my remarks. Malice, Parker. Malign, perverted anger and an urge to destroy, which does not even shrink at the possibility of taking human life in the process. When we get such acts then we begin to find our thoughts directed into other areas. As we progress, so will the motive become clear. But here is the Superintendent back again."

The vigorous figure of Heathfield had returned to the desk, reaching down his raglan overcoat and umbrella from the stand behind it. Behind him stood the uneasy, chastened figure of Sir Clive. Pons turned from the vinegary countenance of the Zoo official and the lid of his right eye dropped slowly. I savoured the moment all the way to the Zoo.

4

It was almost ten o'clock when we arrived at Regent's Park yet despite the lateness of the hour the main entrance to the Zoo was a blaze of light. But the police driver, at a sign from Heathfield, obeyed Sir Clive's instructions to drive farther on to the Fellows' Entrance.

"More discreet," said the President, clearing his throat with an irritating little coughing noise. Pons and I waited until he and Heathfield had alighted and then followed. The rain was still driving hard and I buttoned up my coat collar tightly as we crossed the asphalt. We were within the Zoo grounds as the police car had driven straight in and the coughing roar of a lion, drifting across the Regent Canal came to us, mysterious and sinister in the semi-darkness.

"I have an office in the administrative building," said Sir Clive fussily. "We had best go there initially. I have kept back the key staff following today's incident and you will no doubt wish to question them, Mr. Pons."

"With the Superintendent's permission," said Solar Pons with a slight bow to the Scotland Yard man.

We followed the President through a metal gate and up a path to a large red-brick building set back amid gracious lawns and flower beds. It obviously fronted on to the Inner Circle because I could hear the faint hum of motor traffic from a roadway somewhere beyond. The façade of the building was a blaze of light and the large room into which Sir Clive led us was thronged with chattering groups of officials and attendants in uniform.

A respectful silence fell as we entered and a thin young man with sandy hair detached himself from a knot of people in soberly dressed clothing and hurried toward us.

"Everything is in readiness, Sir Clive."

"Good. This is my secretary, Conrad Foster. Superintendent Heathfield. Mr. Solar Pons. Dr. Lyndon Parker."

The young man nodded pleasantly.

"Welcome, gentlemen. Shall I lead on, sir?"

"By all means. I have just to give some instructions."

The secretary ushered us up a wooden staircase at the side of the building and into Sir Clive's office, a pleasant, simply furnished apartment, evidently one of a number debouching from a long corridor. There were framed photographs of wild animals on the walls, some obviously taken in Africa; and one group included Sir Clive in tropical uniform watching water buffalo through binoculars.

"Please make yourselves comfortable, gentlemen. Sir Clive will not be long."

As he spoke the Zoo chief's tread sounded along the corridor and the little man bounced in and took his place behind the desk, the secretary at his right.

"If you will take notes, Foster, I think we will shortly begin."

He looked at Heathfield and Pons with a quick, bird-like inclination of the head.

"With your permission, gentlemen, I will conduct the preliminary inquiry on today's incident, on behalf of the Society. Naturally you will be free to ask your own questions at any stage of the proceedings. Similarly, any particular member of the staff you require to be questioned can be brought here at short notice." He sniffed, a smug expression on his face. "Though I do not think that will be necessary, as almost everybody who could have the slightest bearing on the matter is waiting down below."

"I see." Superintendent Heathfield nodded, his eye catching Pons with a twinkle. "I cannot speak for Mr. Pons, of course, but that seems perfectly satisfactory to me."

My companion nodded.

"I should like to see the Polar bear enclosure and the body of the animal, if it has not yet been removed, despite the lateness of the hour."

Sir Clive shifted in his chair.

"There will be no difficulty, Mr. Pons. We have our own pathology department here where dead animals are dissected, as well as a well-equipped dispensary for the care of our charges."

"Excellent, Sir Clive," said Solar Pons crisply. "I would also particularly like to have a few words with your Head Keeper, Norman Stebbins, before you begin."

Mortimer looked discomfited.

"But he was not concerned in today's incident, Mr. Pons."

"Exactly, Sir Clive. That is why I wish to see him."

The President turned a little pink around the ears.

"But Mr. Pons, I fail . . . "

"Tut, tut, Sir Clive," said Solar Pons calmly. "It is surely self-evident. Stebbins is in charge of all your staff, is he not? And he obviously knows a good deal about them. I would like him present throughout even if only to corroborate the other attendants' stories. It is vitally important that we have a reliable check on such matters. It will save a good deal of time and can only act in the interests of my client, Hardcastle. Incidentally, I shall require Hardcastle to be present throughout, just as soon as he arrives."

"Very well, Mr. Pons," said Sir Clive grudgingly. "There is a good deal of commonsense in what you say."

"It is good of you to say so," said Solar Pons ironically, evading Superintendent Heathfield's eye. "Now I would suggest we summon Stebbins without more ado."

The Head Keeper proved to be a thickset, muscular man in his early forties with a bright, intelligent face bisected by a heavy brown moustache. He was evidently ill at ease in the presence of the Zoological Society chief but sat down at Pons' request and waited expectantly for the questioning to begin.

Sir Clive opened his mouth to speak but before he could do so my companion cut in smoothly.

"I would just like to ask a few questions, Sir Clive."

"As you wish, Mr. Pons," said the President in a disgruntled voice.

Solar Pons turned to the Head Keeper, tenting his fingers before him.

"That was a first-rate effort at the Lion House, Stebbins. You undoubtedly averted what might have been a major tragedy."

The Head Keeper's face flushed with pleasure.

"It is good of you to say so, Mr. Pons."

Sir Clive cleared his throat.

"The Council has not overlooked the matter, Mr. Pons. A presentation is to be made at a later date."

"I am glad to hear you say so, Sir Clive. A loyal and devoted staff is beyond price in these days of changing values."

Again the annoying throat-clearing by Sir Clive.

"Quite so, Mr. Pons."

Solar Pons turned back to Stebbins.

"Let us just hear your opinion of these strange goings-on."

"Well, sir, begging Sir Clive's pardon, there's not much sense to any of it. Trivial, silly things, like monkey cages being opened. Or windows broken and paint being smeared across buildings. Then the person responsible seems to become enraged and do something dangerous, or even murderous."

Solar Pons chuckled.

"Ah, so you have noticed that have you? I must commend your intelligence. You have no theory to account for it?"

Stebbins shook his head.

"The whole thing is pointless, Mr. Pons, unless a member of the public has a grudge."

"That is what I particularly wanted to ask you, Stebbins. Would access not be difficult for the public?"

An embarrassed look passed across the Head Keeper's face.

"I get your drift, Mr. Pons. I would be loath to suggest that any member of my staff would be responsible. Everyone here loves animals. That goes without saying, or they wouldn't work here."

"Yet dangerous animals have been loosed to kill or maim as they fancy. Is it not so?"

Stebbins nodded reluctantly.

"That is correct, Mr. Pons. But it would not be beyond the bounds for members of the public to gain access to the Zoological Gardens after dark. There are a number of places where an athletic man could get over fences. I would say it seems like the work of an unbalanced person."

An alert expression passed across Solar Pons' feral features.

"What makes you say that?"

Because locks have been smashed on cages where the doors could simply have been opened by the catches. Yet on the cages of dangerous animals such as the tigress, Sheba, or at the Polar bear pit today, heavy padlocks, which one would expect to be smashed have been unlocked as with a key or a picklock."

There was a heavy silence in the room, broken only by the deep-throated roaring of some animal far off across the park. It seemed to give a dark and sinister cast to the subject under discussion.

"That is extremely interesting, Stebbins."

Solar Pons turned to me.

"You may remember, Parker, I told you there is a great deal more here than meets the eye."

"I must confess I am all at sea, Mr. Pons," said the President, obviously non-plussed.

"Nevertheless, we progress, Sir Clive. Our talk here with

your Head Keeper is proving invaluable. He is evidently a man who keeps his eyes open and knows his staff."

"I do my best, sir."

"I am sure you do. You will kindly remain here and give us the benefit of your wisdom when Sir Clive questions the other actors in this strange drama. Ah, here is Hardcastle, none the worse for his little adventure at the Yard."

Indeed, almost before Pons had finished speaking, Hardcastle, his eyes bright and anxious, was sitting down before Sir Clive's desk. That worthy was considerably irritated when Solar Pons calmly rose from his seat.

"I think I have seen and heard enough here for the moment, Sir Clive. We may safely leave this important matter in your hands. As for myself, if Superintendent Heathfield would be so kind, I should like to see the Polar bear enclosure and the other sites of the incidents under examination today."

"Very well, Mr. Pons."

Sir Clive was evidently disgruntled and his face was pink. I saw the secretary Conrad Foster bent over his notebook. He flashed me a secret smile while still turned away from the peppery little man at his side.

Superintendent Heathfield rose and excused himself. Solar Pons nodded affably toward our client.

"Just answer the questions to the best of your ability, Hardcastle, and you will have nothing to fear. Come, Parker."

And he led the way from the room.

5

"But you have learned nothing yet, Pons," I protested as we descended the stairs. "On the contrary, Parker, I have learned a great deal," said my companion, lighting his pipe as we followed the tall form of the Superintendent out into the gardens. The rain had stopped now but the mist persisted and I turned up my coat collar and followed the faint chain of sparks left by Pons' pipe as he hurried forward.

"Sir Clive's examination will lead only to a great deal of repetition. I have already come to some firm conclusions on this affair and would prefer to test them on the ground. I think I can leave it to Stebbins' commonsense to draw to my attention any anomalies in the attendants' statements and no doubt Hardcastle will have his own interests at heart."

"You surprise me, Pons."

"The day I do not, Parker, I shall think my grip is slipping."

"Come, Pons," I said, a little put out. "For instance, what about all these past incidents?"

"Nothing simpler, my dear fellow. I shall visit each site in turn and make my own observations on the spot. The Superintendent has every detail at his finger-tips. And then I shall want to see Hardcastle's lady-friend tomorrow."

"Lady-friend, Pons?"

Solar Pons chuckled as we followed Heathfield through the mist in the direction of the main gate and the Polar bear enclosure.

"The girl, Alice, who warned him that he was under suspicion. She sounds a quick-witted young woman. I have no doubt she will have some ideas of her own about this matter."

"Despite your remarks, Pons, you continue to surprise me."

"Ah, Parker, there is nothing like a woman's intuition in these affairs. Their minds often retain the most surprising information. But here we are at our destination."

We had arrived at Mappin Terrace and Superintendent

Heathfield led the way to the Polar bear enclosures, towering concrete structures, separated from the public by a deep artificial chasm in front of the viewing galleries. We walked up a series of steps to where a group of constables stood with portable electric lights whose thick cables snaked away into the darkness.

Pons hurried forward and examined the heavy padlock and chains which were lying on the ground. A great white form lumbered by in the darkness beyond the bars and I glanced apprehensively at Heathfield. He smiled wryly.

"We are in no danger, Dr. Parker. The Zoo authorities have placed temporary padlocks on this enclosure. The material on the ground here was used to secure the entrance door. It is lying just as it was found."

"Excellent, Superintendent. You have excelled yourself."

Solar Pons bent to one knee. He had his magnifying glass out and examined the lock carefully.

"Opened with a key. You have dusted for prints, I see?"

The Superintendent inclined his head.

"Nothing, Mr. Pons. He was wearing gloves."

Solar Pons smiled at me wryly.

"A cunning fellow, evidently, Parker. But this follows the pattern. Flimsy material smashed. Massive defences unlocked."

"I am sure I do not know what you mean, Pons."

"Just think about it, Parker." My companion turned to the Superintendent. "One bear only was involved?"

"Fortunately, Mr. Pons. The animal was seen moving off down the ramp to the Zoo but was tackled with commendable courage by a junior keeper, Carstairs. He attempted to corner it with a pitchfork, but it attacked and savaged him. The attendants managed to keep it at bay, penning it with rope, hurdles and netting and when my own people arrived they had to shoot it."

"I see." Solar Pons stood in thought for a moment. "It will probably tell us very little but I should like to look at the carcass. Then I think a little visit to the Lion House would be in order, if it can be arranged."

"Certainly, Mr. Pons. Sir Clive has assigned to us a member of the Zoo staff who has most of the master-keys."

"Excellent."

"The corpse of the bear is in the dispensary quarters, Mr. Pons. It is on the way back to the Lion House."

I followed my two companions as they hurried off down toward the Gloucester Gate entrance while a thickset, amiable-looking man in Zoo uniform, evidently the person with the keys mentioned by the Superintendent, followed on behind. Heathfield led the way to a large block of brick buildings which rose from a yard set beside some of the small mammal houses. There was the pungent smell given off by wild animals mingled with disinfectant as we crossed the yard, from which came the sound of a hose-pipe sluicing water over cement.

The corpse of the bear, partly dissected, was lying on a stone slab raised up from the floor under a powerful electric light in a corner of an enormous, bare, whitewashed room.

"I did not think it necessary to have the veterinary surgeons on call tonight, Mr. Pons," said Heathfield.

Solar Pons shook his head.

"They could add nothing and I presume that in any event you have their reports."

"Certainly, Mr. Pons. But with today's near tragedy I felt it essential that we press on with the investigation with the utmost despatch before something more serious occurs."

"It seems difficult to imagine anything more serious," I observed, looking at the huge, blood-stained mass of the bear.

"Polar bears and tigers are serious enough. But I take it you were referring to fatalities."

"Certainly, doctor. It will be only a question of time before this ends in tragedy. The keeper attacked by the bear was badly savaged but is out of danger, I understand."

"Thank heaven for that," I said. "What are your findings there, Pons?"

I went round to stand with my companion as he went over the bear's claws with his powerful lens.

"Precious little, Parker. I did not expect to find anything. But the basic rule of detection is to make a thorough examination, however unlikely it may be to yield anything. One occasionally comes across surprises." He bent over the blood-stained front paws of the colossal beast. "Hullo!" There was excitement in his voice. "What do you make of this, Parker?"

Superintendent Heathfield was standing at the far end of the room now, chatting with the attendant, and we were temporarily alone.

"It looks like a length of thread, Pons."

"Does it not? Perhaps from the uniform of the attacked keeper. However, I think I shall just retain it for the moment. One never knows when it may come in useful."

And he picked out the short length of grey thread and placed it carefully in one of the little envelopes he kept specially for the purpose. The examination was soon concluded and we walked back down toward the Superintendent.

"I take it there is no doubt the Polar bear is a wild and savage animal?"

"None at all, sir," said the attendant, touching his cap to my companion. "Polaris—that's the dead beast, sir, was particularly vicious. Took three shots to kill him."

"Indeed." Solar Pons glanced around him. "Well, Superintendent, I think we have done enough here. I suggest a short visit to the Lion House before we return to Sir Clive." He glanced at his watch. "I think that is all we can hope to do tonight. It will be midnight before we conclude in any event."

Heathfield led the way through the thin mist to where the police car was parked.

"I got Sir Clive's permission. I think it will save time if we go by car and prove less fatiguing. The Zoo grounds are so extensive."

"Admirable, Superintendent. You appear to have thought of everything."

Heathfield smiled thinly and took his place next to the driver while Pons and I and the keeper travelled in the back. After a short interval spent nosing through the mist along the broad asphalt walks between the animal cages, we drew up before the massive entrance of the Victorian Lion House. Lights shone from within the building and there came a low, keening roar that was unmistakable.

We waited while the keeper unlocked the big double doors and followed him into the cavernous interior. A strong odour of the big cats came out to us, bitter and pungent. Dim forms moved behind the bars of the cages set at the left-hand side of the long house and the few overhead lights switched on at this time of night cast deep pools of shadow.

There were stone steps to the right, with wooden benches set on the flat space at the top, and a burly figure in dark uniform was waiting there. He rose as we entered and hurried down the steps toward us. He touched his cap to Superintendent Heathfield whom he had apparently met before.

"Mr. Stebbins told me I was to look out for you, Superintendent. Any way in which I can help..."

"Thank you," said Heathfield crisply. "We may need you shortly. For the moment we will just look about."

The burly man saluted again and went back to the bench with his colleague and their gloomy conversation came down to us from time to time as we walked on in front of the great beasts. Pons himself reminded me of nothing so much as the inmates of the cages as he prowled restlessly about, darting sharp glances here and there.

"Which is the cage from which Sheba escaped, Superintendent?"

"This one here, Mr. Pons."

Heathfield had stopped before a large enclosure set about halfway down the spacious house, in which a magnificent tigress paced majestically up and down, every now and then giving vent to a low, rumbling growl. Solar Pons paused and gazed thoughtfully into the great beast's glowing yellow eyes.

"A magnificent sight, Heathfield. I know of nothing so impressive. Intelligence, strength and courage. A formidable combination."

"Indeed, Mr. Pons. So you can imagine the degree of determination on Stebbins' part in acting as he did in preventing the beast from escaping."

"The point had not eluded me, Superintendent. I must examine the main door before I leave. In the meantime, with your permission, I will just have a look at this cage here."

To my alarm he eased his lithe, angular form over the low metal barrier to prevent the public from approaching too close to the cages and bent down in the narrow gangway inside. The tigress immediately stopped her pacing and then flung herself against the bars of the cage in an absolute paroxysm of fury. The sight was so stupendous in its savagery and the noise so deafening that even Pons was momentarily diverted from his purpose.

"What an incredible beast, Pons."

"Is she not, Parker."

"Take care, Pons."

"I shall certainly do that, Parker."

The animal was silent again now and resumed her tireless pacing, though every now and then she cast a sullen glare on my companion from her smouldering yellow eyes. The two keepers had come forward from the terrace at the back and now stood by silently, the burly man fingering a long metal pole.

"I do not think that will be necessary," said Solar Pons with a thin smile.

He bent forward to look at the cage, which had a sliding door, the bar of which was secured by a strong padlock.

"Has this been changed, do you know, Superintendent?"

Heathfield shook his head.

"Not to my knowledge, Mr. Pons. It had been opened with a key, according to our experts, and the retaining bar slid back."

"A risky business," said Solar Pons drily, turning his gaze up toward the ceiling. "Hullo!" There was a sharp urgency in his voice.

"What is it, Mr. Pons?"

"Look there."

We all followed Solar Pons' pointing finger. At first I could not make it out and then saw a small piece of frayed twine which was fastened to the bars of the sliding door near the top.

"Just a piece of string, Pons."

"Is it not, Parker! But a simple ruse which ensured the survival of this Phantom you talk about. Unless I mistake my vocation he simply attached a cord and slid the door open from the safety of that door yonder."

He turned to the keepers.

"What is in there?"

"Feed-store and staff locker-room, sir."

"Hmm."

Solar Pons climbed back over the barrier and rejoined us, his eyes sharp and intent, oblivious of the caged forms of the lions and tigers which circled aimlessly in the background.

"The twine may have been broken by the tigress when she jumped to the ground. Perhaps by a hind leg. Or our man may simply have snapped it with a strong tug. How would he have got out?"

"There is another door to the outside beyond the locker-room, Mr. Pons," said the burly keeper, looking at my companion curiously.

"What is your name?"

"Hodgson, sir."

"Very well, Hodgson, just lead on, will you?"

The thickset keeper walked briskly up to the far door and beckoned us through into a chill, high, bleak room which seemed cold despite the bales of straw in the corner. There was a heavy wooden block with a cleaver and saw; the remains of a carcass on it; and some metal bins for foodstuffs.

"This is where you prepare the food for the animals?" said Pons, glancing round him keenly.

"Exactly, sir."

The Lion House was well-heated and I suppose it was the contrast between it and this chill place which made me glad to quit it as Hodgson opened another door at the rear. This led to a small, cheerful room equipped with a gas fire; some tables and chairs; a stove; and a section in the corner where there were rows of green-painted lockers.

"This is our recreation room, sir. Cosy enough," said our informant with a sniff, looking about him. We all stood silent for a bit as Solar Pons paced round the room, his sharp glance appearing to miss nothing.

He stopped before the lockers with a grunt and produced his powerful pocket magnifying lens.

"Which of these is Hardcastle's?"

"Number Four, sir," said Hodgson, with a puzzled look on his face.

"It is unlocked?"

"Certainly, sir. None of them lock."

"I just wondered," said Solar Pons blandly. "As I see this one in the corner has a length of wire twisted through the hasp."

"That's mine, sir," replied Hodgson, a flush appearing on his features. "I am in charge here you see, sir."

"And you prefer a little privacy. Of course, Hodgson. I am not implying any criticism. All the same I would like each of the lockers opened."

Hodgson glanced at Superintendent Heathfield for a moment and then went forward with ill grace, untwisting the strands of wire. In the meantime Pons had opened Hardcastle's locker and was busy with its contents.

"Where is the material you removed from here, Superintendent?"

"It has been sealed in Sir Clive's office, Mr. Pons."

Pons nodded.

"It is no matter, really. Paint, an axe, gloves and other items, I believe."

"Yes, Mr. Pons. I have the list here."

Pons studied it in silence, then went swiftly round the other lockers, cursorily examining their contents.

"We tested for prints, Mr. Pons," Heathfield volunteered.

"But found nothing useful," said Solar Pons with a thin smile. "Because everyone who works in or comes and goes from the Lion House has been along this aisle or put their hands against these lockers from time to time."

"Exactly, Mr. Pons. The whole situation was too confused and we could read nothing from it."

"I am not surprised."

Hodgson had opened the door of his locker now and stood aside. As he did so a small piece of pasteboard fluttered to the ground.

"Allow me."

Solar Pons had stooped and picked it up before the other could move.

"What a charming young girl."

He held up the picture between thumb and forefinger, watching the slow flush which suffused the keeper's features.

"My young lady, sir."

Hodgson took the picture from Pons and put it quickly in his pocket.

"My congratulations."

Pons glanced swiftly into the interior of the locker which contained nothing of any great interest so far as I could make out.

"Thank you, Hodgson. I do not think there is anything further for the moment."

And with that he led the way to the door which communicated with the open air.

6

"Well, Parker, what are your views on the affair?"

I braced myself in the interior of the cab, which had just lurched to a shuddering stop in a traffic jam, and regarded Pons quizzically. It was a cold, misty morning, though the rain had stopped, and we were on our way to the Zoological Gardens for a conference with Sir Clive and Heathfield.

Pons had remained closed with Heathfield and the Zoo officials until a late hour the previous evening, collating testimony from the various zoo staff, and I must confess I had dozed off in my corner of the office in which I had begged to be left. Pons had been in an extremely pensive mood on our way back to Praed Street and his uncommunicativeness had prevailed throughout breakfast this morning so that I was pleased to see his normal mood restored.

"I am all at sea, Pons."

"You do yourself an injustice, Parker. Pray apply your mind to it."

I settled myself more comfortably in my corner as our driver started off again at a more decorous rate and stared at Pons through the haze of pipe-smoke.

"There is a good deal here I do not understand."

Solar Pons smiled quizzically.

"Ah, then we are at one, Parker. It is indeed a fascinating problem. Or rather problems. Though I am on the way to solving one the major eludes me."

I stared at my companion in astonishment.

"Indeed, Pons. It sounds remarkable."

"It is remarkable, Parker. And quite unique. And if I do not miss my guess we have not yet got properly into the case."

I fear my mouth must have dropped open but I did not have time for further talk as the cab was drawing up in front of a pleasant, red-brick house.

"Here we are, Parker. Sir Clive's private residence."

The handsome mansion which composed itself before us out of the mist had tall iron gates separating it from the Inner Circle and as we walked up the paved path between twin lawns, we could see that another path led away to a further iron gate at the rear, which evidently communicated with the Zoo grounds.

"Grace and favour, Pons," I remarked.

Solar Pons smiled thinly.

"'You have hit it exactly, Parker. Such sinecures are apt to lead to jealousy in the somewhat esoteric world of zoology as much as elsewhere."

We had stopped at the imposing porch, where Pons rang the bell, and I stared at him quizzically.

"You are not suggesting that a professional rival is attempting to discredit Sir Clive's direction of the Zoological Gardens?"

"Such things have happened before, Parker. Young Hardcastle may have got into deeper waters than he imagines. However, I should be able to set his mind at rest when we meet later this morning. He resumes his duties today, does he not?"

"Thanks to you, Pons. But will it not provide the real criminal—for these are criminal acts going on here—with a golden opportunity?"

"There is method in my madness, Parker."

And with that I had to be content. A parlour-maid speedily showed us to a light-panelled, pleasant room on the ground floor where Sir Clive and Heathfield were already ensconced. The Head Keeper, Stebbins, evidently ill at ease in such surroundings, stood awkwardly on the rug in front of the fire and twisted his peaked cap in his hands.

As we came in a fourth man I had not seen rose from a large wing-chair set next to the fire.

"It is outrageous!" he spluttered. "It is discrediting the Society!"

He paused as he became aware of our approach.

"This is hardly the time or the place for such a discussion, Jefferies," said Sir Clive blandly. "We will continue it some other time, if you please." The tall man in the dark frock-coat and with the white mane of hair which made him look like a musician bowed stiffly. "This is a colleague of mine on the Council of the Zoological Society," said the President with a thin-lipped smile. "Gordon Jefferies. Mr. Solar Pons. Dr. Lyndon Parker."

Jefferies bowed icily, raking us with insolent eyes.

"Your servant, gentlemen. Good-day, Mortimer."

He nodded brusquely and swept out followed by the ironic eyes of Sir Clive.

"A detestable man, Mr. Pons," he muttered *sotto voce*. "But brilliant in his field. He has many enemies."

"Indeed," said Solar Pons, with a shrewd look at our host. "So I should imagine if he carries on in such a manner. What was the trouble?"

"My handling of the current crisis in the Society's affairs," said Sir Clive. "Though to tell the truth he is put out because he feels he has not been kept fully informed by the Council.

But he has made large donations to funds and so feels he partly owns the Zoological Gardens."

He chuckled drily and seemed in jocular mood, despite the obvious altercation that had just taken place.

He looked a dapper figure in his well-cut grey suit and I saw that Pons was studying him carefully beneath his apparently casual manner.

Sir Clive waved us to chairs near the fire where a silver-plated coffee pot and cups were set out.

"But he is a brilliant person, nevertheless," he continued. "And has made some original contributions to biology. A specialist in the habits of the gorilla."

"Indeed," said Solar Pons again. "I hope he finds their company a little more congenial. He certainly seemed to look with disfavour upon Parker and myself."

Superintendent Heathfield smiled.

"You have not yet heard his fulminations upon the ineptitude of the official police, Mr. Pons."

Solar Pons returned his smile.

"That would have been worth hearing, eh, Parker? Come, Stebbins. Have a cup of coffee and sit down yonder. Sir Clive will not eat you."

"Thank you, Mr. Pons. You are very kind."

The Head Keeper sat down gingerly on a straight-backed chair opposite, though it was evident by the frosty expression on Sir Clive's face that he did not approve of this breach of social etiquette.

When we all had a cup in our hands, Sir Clive pulled round his armchair to favour the fire and said fussily, "We must plan our campaign, Mr. Pons."

"By all means, Sir Clive. I have already travelled far in my conclusions."

Sir Clive raised his eyebrows and blew his cheeks in and out once or twice.

"May we be favoured with them, Mr. Pons?"

Solar Pons pulled reflectively at the lobe of his left ear.

"It is a little too early for the present. I would like to hear your own views on the person—or persons—who have been carrying out these outrages at the Zoo. Shorn of all emotional bias, of course."

Sir Clive looked sourly at my companion and then round at the faces of Superintendent Heathfield and Stebbins. He shuffled a bundle of papers he held in his hands.

"These are my conclusions, Mr. Pons. The depositions of the staff members concerned in this weird business. Plus my reasoned notes on the matter."

Solar Pons smiled bleakly.

"Save them for the Council and the Society's official journals, Sir Clive. It would take us all day to go through those. Pray be more selective."

Sir Clive's face turned purple and Heathfield had a sudden choking attack which he cured by an instant draught of coffee. Sir Clive drew his lips into a thin line and glared at me instead.

"Very well, Mr. Pons. A disgruntled former employee of the Zoo, perhaps. We have had occasion to discharge three within the past two years."

Solar Pons looked interrogatively at the military figure of the Superintendent.

"It is a possibility, Sir Clive," he said reluctantly. "Let us hear what the Superintendent has to say."

Heathfield shook his head.

"We have already checked, Mr. Pons. One man has gone abroad; the other two live far out of London."

"They have been questioned?"

"Oh yes. There is no doubt that they are in the clear."

Solar Pons' piercing eyes rested briefly on Stebbins.

"All the same I should like to have Mr. Stebbins' opinion."

The burly Head Keeper shook his head.

"This business has nothing to do with them, Mr. Pons, that I'll swear. They haven't the character for a business like this. A nasty mind is behind this, Mr. Pons."

"I am inclined to agree with you, Stebbins," said Solar Pons languidly. "What do you think of young Hardcastle, now?"

The Head Keeper shook his head again, more doggedly than before.

"I can't believe it, Mr. Pons. The Zoo has never had a more loyal employee among the uniformed staff."

"You make a distinction, then?"

Stebbins looked sharply at Pons.

"I speak as I find, sir. The uniformed staff come under my jurisdiction. I have no knowledge of the scientific, clerical and other personnel. Even if I had it would not be my place to criticise."

Sir Clive had little pink spots on his cheeks.

"Well said, Stebbins," said Solar Pons warmly. "I am sure I shall find your advice invaluable." He looked at his watch. "If you have no objection, Sir Clive, I would like to see the rest of the cages and houses where the other incidents took place. Then a little lunch would not come amiss."

"Certainly, Mr. Pons. There is an excellent restaurant in the Zoo grounds. You would be welcome to partake of my hospitality here. Or the Fellows' Restaurant could be put at your disposal."

"It is too good of you, Sir Clive," said Solar Pons, rising to his feet. "But we have already caused considerable disruption in your routine. If Parker has no objection, I would prefer to lunch at the public restaurant at a time which suits. Will you join us, Superintendent?"

"Certainly, Mr. Pons."

"That is settled, then. Shall we say half-past one? Come, Parker."

And Solar Pons led the way out of the room so swiftly that I was hard put to keep up with him.

7

"Ah, there you are, Hardcastle!"

The shadows had lifted from our client's face and now he hurried toward us down the length of the Lion House, a slim, fair-haired girl at his heels. It was late afternoon and after an excellent lunch Pons and I had spent an hour with Heathfield, touring the houses where the other incidents had taken place.

"Allow me to introduce my fiancée, Miss Alice Westover, Mr. Pons."

"Delighted, Miss Westover."

Pons glanced at the girl and then his gaze rested briefly on the knots of thickly-clad people who had gathered in the warmth of the Lion House to see the animals.

"You have a fair crowd for such a day, I see."

"Average, Mr. Pons. The big cats attract the public at almost any time of the year."

"So I should imagine."

Pons looked the girl in the eye.

"What do you think of all this, Miss Westover?"

The girl moved protectively toward the young keeper and linked her arm through his.

"He is certainly innocent, Mr. Pons," she said stoutly.

Solar Pons looked at her reflectively, noting the smart tailored suit and the chic hat with its gaily-coloured feathers.

"You are most loyal, Miss Westover. But in any event I do not think there is much doubt of your fiancé's innocence."

"I am glad to hear it from your own lips, Mr. Pons," the girl said gravely.

We had moved unconsciously down the great hall, where the restless denizens continued their tireless pacing and Pons stared rather pointedly at the girl I thought. Though Hardcastle was oblivious of my companion's scrutiny, it was not lost upon his companion, who had little points of fire dancing on her cheeks.

"Have you heard anything, Mr. Pons?"

"We progress, Hardcastle, we progress."

"I cannot rest, Mr. Pons, until this stigma is removed from my good name."

"Have patience, Hardcastle. We shall soon be at the root of the matter." Pons looked up sharply. "Ah, there is Hodgson. I think he wants you, Hardcastle."

The girl bit her lip and flushed as Hardcastle hurried down the Lion House to where the burly figure of the senior Keeper stood. From what I could make out they seemed to be arguing about something.

"Your fiancé and Hodgson do not get on very well, I think," said Solar Pons shrewdly, his deep-set eyes studying the girl's face.

"I really do not know, Mr. Pons."

"Do you not, Miss Westover?"

I moved away a little awkwardly and stood back a few feet, almost out of earshot, until Pons motioned me across.

There is nothing private about this, Parker. I wish you to hear."

"As you please, Pons. Though I must confess I am all at sea."

"Nevertheless, Parker, I would prefer you to stay. We may talk unobserved in this corner. Jealousy is a dreadful thing, Miss Westover. It may provoke all sorts of unexpected events. Including violence born of frustrated rage."

The girl's face turned white. She looked over Pons' shoulder toward the far end of the Lion House where the two keepers were still engrossed in conversation. She turned back to my companion.

"You know something, Mr. Pons?"

"Let us say I suspect something, Miss Westover. Something involving you and Hardcastle and Hodgson. Am I right?"

The girl bit her lip again.

"There was no harm in it, Mr. Pons," she said sullenly. "Though I do not know how you could have guessed."

"Intuition combined with sharp eyesight, Miss Westover. I have no doubt you saw no harm in it, but great harm has flowed from it."

The girl's eyes were open and tears glimmered on her lashes.

"I don't know what you are talking about, Mr. Pons."

Solar Pons shook his head.

"That is certainly true, my dear young lady. But I advise you to break off the association without delay as the man concerned will shortly be in considerable trouble." He put his fingers to his lips. "Your fiancé is coming back, Miss Westover. Absolute discretion?"

The girl nodded, her face still white.

"Absolute discretion, Mr. Pons. And thank you."

Solar Pons smiled thinly.

"Learn to profit by the experience, Miss Westover. I am an

excellent judge of human nature and you will not do better than young Hardcastle."

And saluting the pair of them, for Hardcastle had now come up with us, he moved away toward the entrance of the Lion House. As soon as we were out of earshot I caught him by the arm.

"What on earth was all that about, Pons?"

"Just a little well-meant advice, Parker. I think the young lady will have profited by the lesson."

"I wish I knew what you were talking about, Pons," I grumbled.

"Patience, Parker, patience. All will be explained in due course. But I must confess that one thing still puzzles me. I now have two distinct strands but no possible motive for the second." Solar Pons paused and looked at my thunderstruck face before bursting into laughter. "Really, Parker, your features present an indescribable picture! But it is almost dusk. I suggest we use the passes with which Sir Clive has furnished us and remain in the grounds until after dark. Let us just give it an hour. Perhaps we can spend the time in one of the heated tropical houses because the night promises to be cold."

We were outside now and the air was indeed biting.

"But what on earth are we going to do, Pons?"

My companion stared at me, his lean, feral features alight with excitement.

"I have the feeling that something that should have happened has not yet happened. Call it a sixth sense if you will. But I am rarely wrong. A number of incidents have occurred, some trivial, some serious. In my opinion they are but stage-dressing for something else." My puzzlement must have been evident on my features for Pons slowed his walk and looked at me with wry affection. "My dear Parker, I do not know what will happen or where danger will strike. The Zoo grounds are large and extensive, the houses and animal enclosures numerous and complicated. But I should feel more at ease if you would stay with me for an hour or two."

"Certainly, Pons," said I. "But if we are going to hang about in the cold I suggest we first repair to the restaurant or the Fellows' dining room. There is an excellent bar there and I have a first-rate prescription for keeping out the cold."

Solar Pons chuckled.

"There are unsuspected depths to you, Parker. Sometimes it is difficult to remember you are a physician."

And with which sardonic comment he set off at a brisk pace across the grounds.

8

Mist swirled silently in the darkness and far off a faint gas-lamp sent out a drowning beam of light toward us. The coughing roar of a lion echoed, melancholy and remote across the park, and left a sombre reflection in my heart. I shifted my feet and stamped them cautiously, conscious of Pons' disapproving face beside me in the gloom. We stood in the deep porch of one of the mammal houses and rested briefly. We had been walking about the Zoological Gardens for an hour but it seemed as though we had covered miles. I was about to venture an observation when Pons' hand was upon my arm and I heard the hissed intake of his breath.

A moment later I caught the sound which his sharp ears had already heard: the agitated beat of a man's feet running through the white blanket. It was far off and for a moment I could not place the direction. Then we both caught the urgent note of the voice. There was fear and panic in it as it called, "Murder! Police!"

Pons gave a muffled exclamation.

"We are too late, Parker! I blame myself for this. As quick as you can."

He was already disappearing into the fog and I had difficulty in keeping his tall, lean figure in sight. He moved fast, despite the whiteness which hemmed us in, and his sharp eyes unerringly guided us round obstructions and kept us in the right direction.

Within two minutes we could hear the muffled sound of more footsteps in response to urgent calls and figures were about us. A police constable lurched into me, his bulls-eye lantern making a pale glow, and recoiled with an apology.

"Dr. Parker isn't it? Up near the next entrance, sir."

When Pons and I arrived, there was a small knot of people, and the purposeful figure of Superintendent Heathfield detached itself from the *mêlée*.

"Good to see you both, Mr. Pons. It is fatal this time, I am afraid. In the gorilla enclosure."

Solar Pons nodded, his face impassive and dream-like in the light of the lanterns.

"That has solved one mystery, Superintendent."

The words were spoken almost to himself and I saw the police officer look at him with a start. With the frightened attendant who had given the alarm leading the way, we were soon at the scene of the tragedy. It had taken place in a large wood and cement building which housed the greater primates. The main door had been broken, the glass panel shattered.

The leading attendants and the uniformed police officers were pressing inside when Pons stopped them with a sudden exclamation.

"Hullo! This is curious indeed, Parker. The glass has been broken from inside."

Heathfield and I exchanged puzzled glances. Pons had stooped to examine the shattered fragments of glass which lay on the cement walk outside the entrance.

"That is so, Mr. Pons. Why on earth would anyone want to break out?"

Solar Pons smiled an enigmatic smile.

"Think about it, my dear fellow. It leads to one inescapable conclusion."

"Perhaps, Pons," I said shortly. "But can we not leave this until later? It is cold out here and if murder has been done inside..."

"You are quite right, Parker. Lead on, Superintendent."

I hurried in the wake of my companions and in a few moments more we came upon one of the most bizarre and horrific scenes I had ever encountered either during my years with Pons or within my medical experience.

The house was divided into two parts with a broad cement aisle separating the heated enclosures either side. Chimpanzees, gibbons and large apes sat sullenly in their respective cages, blinking in the dim electric light, as though they had been awakened from sleep. There was a welcome warmth in here and I guessed that the stout metal walls at the rear of the cages, each complete with sliding door, gave on to roomy enclosures in the open air which the animals occupied in summer.

The attendant who had raised the alarm was standing by a large, thickly barred enclosure at the far end of the house; a dim form loomed gigantically within and made shuffling noises in the deep straw and other litter which covered the floor. A constable near me shone his electric lantern within the bars and disclosed the dark-clad human figure which lay at a grotesque angle. Motionless and rigid it was a foot or two from the indistinct shape.

Then the lantern beam moved upward and I could not repress a shudder as its rays caught the red-rimmed eyes; the crooked teeth; and the black, bestial muzzle. The huge gorilla stared unwinkingly at the spectators beyond the bars while its claws continued to make shuffling noises in the straw. I pulled my eyes reluctantly away from that terrific spectacle.

"You are the expert, Parker," said Pons coolly. "Pray give us your opinion."

I looked again at the form which sprawled face down, its features invisible in the littered straw.

"He is undoubtedly dead, Pons," I said. "The angle of the head indicates that immediately. His neck has been broken."

"Has it not. I had come to roughly the same conclusion myself but I am glad to have your professional opinion. Under the circumstances it is perhaps just as well, as it will undoubtedly take some little time to extricate the body." He glanced up at the white plaque which was attached to the wall near the cage. "Boris. Male Gorilla. Hmm. What do you make of it, Superintendent?"

"I would not like to express an *ad hoc* opinion, Mr. Pons, but it certainly looks as though the intruder gained entrance to the beast's cage with the intention of letting it loose. We may have inadvertently discovered the Phantom."

"It could be so," said Solar Pons carelessly. "But I have grave doubts."

He indicated the sliding bolt on the door. The padlock and chain lay on the floor but the bolt had been slid to.

"It is hardly likely that he would secure the door behind him under those circumstances. And I understood the gorilla was a vegetarian."

"That is correct, sir," the attendant volunteered. "Can't understand it. Boris is as gentle as a lamb"

"Indeed," said Solar Pons, looking thoughtfully at the great beast, whose eyes stared so soulfully into our own. "It is a pity he cannot talk, Parker. There is certainly great intelligence there. I could almost swear that he is as puzzled as yourself as to how a corpse came into his cage." Solar Pons gazed at the attendant from the Gorilla House for a long moment. "Why did you call out 'Murder', just now?"

The man looked startled.

"The person in the cage was obviously dead, sir. His neck's all twisted. I said the first thing that came into my head. And I wanted to get help urgently."

"I see. But why could it not have been an accident?"

The man shook his head stubbornly.

"Not an accident, sir. No one in his senses would go into that cage."

"So you do not think the gorilla killed him?"

"No, sir. I've been in charge of Boris for fifteen years. He's gentle and even tempered and there are several of us can go into his cage without any trouble."

"That is interesting!"

Solar Pons turned back to the bars as the keeper approached the door. We stood clear as he slid back the bolt and spoke to the gorilla in a low, crooning tone. The great shambling form backed away. The attendant bent gently and seized the figure of the fallen man by the foot nearest the door. He dragged the body slowly toward us. I bent to aid him. With the help of a police constable we pulled the body out and the attendant shut the door.

I bent and turned over the figure in the frock-coat. I could not resist a gasp of surprise. We all stood staring down at the dead face of Gordon Jefferies, while a sudden clamour of animal noise, savage and muted, swept across the park from outside. Solar Pons looked at Superintendent Heathfield sombrely.

"An expert on gorillas, I believe. Murder it is."

9

Sir Clive's face was ashen and distorted with anger. "This is appalling, Superintendent. I demand that the culprit be brought to book immediately."

"We are doing our best, Sir Clive."

"It is not good enough, Superintendent. Really, Mr. Pons."

Solar Pons paused in the act of lighting his pipe, the ruddy glow from the bowl stippling his lean, ascetic face with little points of fire. He smiled disarmingly.

"Do not let me interrupt you, Sir Clive. But it is difficult to see what the London Police could have done to prevent this. It was carefully planned."

"Eigh?"

Sir Clive's eyes were round and he looked at my companion suspiciously. We were sitting in Sir Clive's office and round the desk, in addition to Stebbins, the Head Keeper, were our client, Hardcastle; Hodgson; the secretary, Conrad Foster; and several other senior keepers. In the background were two grave-faced, soberly dressed gentlemen, fellow members of Sir Clive's on the Council of the Zoological Society; and several high-ranking plain-clothes men of the C.I.D. who were sitting in on the conference.

It was nine o'clock in the evening and despite the refreshment we had taken in the Fellows' Restaurant I was feeling tired and hungry. Oily fog swirled at the windows of the large office and the air was blue with stale tobacco smoke. The inquiry had gone on for nearly two hours but so far as I could see the protagonists were no nearer coming to any conclusions regarding the murder of Gordon Jefferies.

Except Pons, of course. He had listened quietly to the argument and had so far not ventured an opinion. Now he drew steadily on his pipe until it was burning to his satisfaction and tented his long, thin fingers together in front of him.

"Would you mind explaining, Mr. Pons?"

Sir Clive's eyes were full of curiosity.

"In due course, sir. I say it was carefully planned. The murderer cunningly took advantage of fortuitous circumstances. One might say that the occasion was tailor-made. And the popular press reports of a Phantom in the Zoo could not have suited him better."

There was an ugly silence and I could see the uniformed attendants looking uneasily at one another.

"I do not follow you, Mr. Pons."

It was Superintendent Heathfield on this occasion. Solar Pons shrugged his thin shoulders.

"I hope to name the murderer for you before the evening is out, Superintendent. It is only a question of time."

"Pons!" I exclaimed. "You do not mean to say you know his name?"

"I have strong suspicions, Parker. It is one thing to theorise; another to prove beyond a conclusive doubt."

There was an air of electric tension in the room now. Sir Clive shifted uncomfortably in his chair and sought support from his Council colleagues in the back row. Before he could speak again Solar Pons sat up in his chair next to Sir Clive's desk and nodded affably over toward Hardcastle.

"Perhaps you would care to tell Sir Clive and the assembled company exactly how you broke into the cages and wrought your trail of mischief?"

Hardcastle was on his feet, his face working.

"I am innocent, Mr. Pons," he stammered.

"Tut," said Solar Pons calmly. "Pray sit down. We do not need such exhibitions. I was referring to friend Hodgson there behind you."

I stared in amazement at the burly figure of the Keeper of the Lion House, who seemed visibly to crumble. He started up, guilt evident upon his face.

"I do not know what you are talking about, Mr. Pons!"

"I think you do, Hodgson. Red paint is very difficult to remove from the finger-nails. I noticed specks of it beneath your nails when I spoke to you at the Lion House this afternoon. I made it my business to inquire of the zoo staff. No red paint has been used on the animal cages lately. Except for the vandal who daubed the mammal houses. And placed the materials in the locker of Hardcastle here."

Superintendent Heathfield was on his feet, his face stern.

"Is this true, Hodgson?"

The big keeper had collapsed now; he sat with his head in his hands. Then he raised an ashen face to stare at Pons.

"I admit it, Mr. Pons," he said. "But murder, no."

"We shall see," said Solar Pons coldly.

"But what possible motive could he have, Pons?" I asked.

"Jealousy," said Solar Pons across the rising murmur of voices within the room. "Plain, ordinary jealousy. I am sorry to say it, Hardcastle, but Hodgson was jealous of your success with Miss Westover."

"Mr. Pons!"

There was dismay on the young man's face.

"My attention was directed to it quite accidentally. When I asked Hodgson to open his locker he had a photograph there which fell to the ground. I saw the young lady's face quite clearly when I picked it up. When you introduced me to your fiancée later I saw quite plainly it was she. A few veiled questions and her obvious confusion soon made me see how the land lay. Hodgson hoped to secure your dismissal and secure the young lady's affections for himself, unless I am very much mistaken."

Hardcastle swore and plunged toward Hodgson but the plain-clothes officers were too quick for him and interposed themselves. Handcuffs flashed and the burly keeper was securely pinioned.

"There will be time enough for recriminations later," said Solar Pons mildly. "Am I not right, Hodgson?"

"Yes, sir," said the big keeper sullenly. "I broke into the cages, let the animals loose and did that damage. I put the things in Hardcastle's locker and hoped to lose him his job. It was my feelings for the young lady that made me do it. I'm sorry now. We'd been out a few times and then she threw me over for Hardcastle. I hoped to get her back. And I'd been out with her a few times since. My pay was better than his, you see, and I had good prospects. But I know nothing about the murder of Mr. Jefferies."

"That remains to be seen," said Superintendent Heathfield calmly. He turned to my companion. "I am in your debt, Mr. Pons."

"Think nothing of it, Superintendent," said Solar Pons, a strange look in his eyes. "My reward lies in clearing Hardcastle here from all stigma."

"Take him away. We will finish questioning him at the Yard."

Heathfield bustled forward and the groups seated round the desk broke up. Sir Clive came forward and pumped Pons by the hand.

"A remarkable performance, my dear sir. I am most grateful."

"It was nothing, Sir Clive."

Pons hastily excused himself and we strode back down the staircase and into the fog.

"There are one or two points I don't quite understand, Pons."

To my astonishment Solar Pons put his hand over my mouth and drew me into the deep shadow of one of the mammal houses.

"Not a word, Parker. And pray do not be idiotic. The case is far from over. We must secure our man while he is still off-balance. Follow me and be careful in this fog."

And before I had time to convey my astonishment and chagrin my companion was dragging me through the white blanket until my sense of direction was entirely lost.

Presently the dark, skeletal bars of an iron gate loomed up in the mist. It was unlocked and Pons pushed it back to enable us to slip through, carefully closing it behind us. He led me unerringly down a flagged path toward the massive structure of a large mansion from which shaded lights glowed.

"What on earth, Pons?" I began. "This is Sir Clive's residence..."

"I am well aware of that, Parker," Solar Pons whispered. "Now, if I am not much mistaken, the study should be here."

He cast about him, looking intently at marks on the grass verge. Apparently satisfied, he tiptoed across the lawn toward French windows which, to judge from the darkness within, denoted an unoccupied room. I had no choice but to accompany him but I was filled with horror when Pons produced a metal instrument from his pocket and calmly inserted it into the lock.

"You are surely not going to break in, Pons?"

"It is quite illegal, Parker, but the short answer is yes," Pons replied imperturbably. "This is one advantage we have over Scotland Yard, Parker. They do not normally break into citizens' private houses. With the result that some damnable villains are allowed to go free."

"But what do you expect to find, Pons?"

"Nothing, Parker, unless I can deal with this lock. Let us hope there are no bolts or I shall have to risk smashing a pane."

There was a sudden click as he spoke and he gave a soft exclamation of satisfaction. One wing of the door was open and he beckoned me to follow as he eased himself slowly through into the darkness. I followed and shut the door quietly behind me, being brought up against thick velvet curtains. Pons cautiously slid them back a few inches and I could see by the soft glow of a dying log fire that we were within a comfortably furnished study.

"What are we going to do, Pons?"

"Just wait patiently, Parker. Our man will not be long. We may catch him off-guard. Unless I miss my guess he has not yet finished disposing of the evidence. I have no doubt he has already used these windows tonight."

"I am completely lost, Pons. I thought that Hodgson..."

"Hush, Parker."

Solar Pons' strong grip made me wince as he caught my arm. I then heard the crisp sound of footsteps along the flagged walk of the garden outside. A minute or so passed and the crash of the front door was followed by muffled voices. Pons put his finger to his lips and pulled the curtains back across the alcove in which we were standing.

We had not long to wait. Hardly had we concealed ourselves before there was the grate of a key in the lock of the study door and the room was flooded with light, the golden glow which penetrated the curtains enabling me to see that Pons had his eye fastened to a faint crack through which he surveyed the room. I passed the time with what patience I could muster though I must confess that the police and the laws of private property were much in my mind.

I joined Pons at his urgent motioning and saw what had attracted his attention. Putting my eye to the gap in the curtains, which Pons held closed with his right hand, I could see the portly form of Sir Clive. He was down on his knees by a large desk, examining the floor. Then he got up and crossed over to a small safe set into the fireplace wall. He took from it a bundle of documents and placed them on the desk. Then he went back into the middle of the room in a listening attitude.

He turned to the fireplace and picked up a poker. He sifted the dying fire and I heard a muffled exclamation. He went over to a scuttle at the side of the hearth apparently to find it empty.

"We are in luck, Parker," Pons breathed in my ear.

Sir Clive hesitated a moment longer, glanced at the documents on the desk and then picked up the scuttle. He passed out of my line of vision and I heard the sound of the catch as the door was opened. The key sounded again as he locked it from the other side and his footsteps died away.

"Excellent, Parker," Solar Pons chuckled. "There will never be a better opportunity."

He ran across the room without any attempt at concealment and I followed with considerable misgiving. Pons was already down on his hands and knees, examining the floor with his lens.

"He will need a cloth too," he murmured.

"What exactly is happening, Pons?"

"Sir Clive is about to burn these letters. We must just glance at them, for the motive is not yet clear to me."

He picked them up, his face turning grave as he leafed through them. He replaced them on the desk.

"Poor devil."

He stood in thought for a moment.

"Blackmail is one of the vilest of crimes, Parker, and I am not so sure the punishment was not justified in this case. But murder is frowned on by the authorities and we must not be deflected from our purpose."

And he stood calmly by the mantelpiece, lighting his pipe

and staring down at the almost extinguished fire until footsteps again sounded on the parquet of the hall outside. We were still standing like that when Sir Clive entered, locked the door behind him and advanced toward the fireplace, bearing fresh billets of wood in his scuttle. There was a tremendous clatter as he dropped it, the iron bucket overturning and scattering the wood about the polished floor. He stood before us with a deathly face, guilt staring from every lineament of his features.

"Mr. Pons!" he cried in a croaking voice, all the arrogance gone from his tones. "What does this mean?"

"It means, Sir Clive, that all is known," said Solar Pons equably, lighting his pipe and puffing blue columns of smoke toward the carved ceiling, the firelight glowing on his lean, ascetic features.

If the President's face had been haggard before, the change in it was so dramatic that I feared he might have a stroke. He made a choking noise and I hurried forward to assist him to a chair by the fire. I loosened his collar and handed him a glass of brandy which Pons poured from a decanter on the desk.

"I am sorry to subject you to this, Sir Clive," said Pons, when the recumbent man's face had assumed a more healthful colour. "But there was no other way."

Sir Clive turned burning eyes to my companion.

"How did you know, Mr. Pons?"

"There were two distinct patterns to the strange events at the Zoological Gardens. One set was distinctly trivial while the others were serious. One featured senseless damage; the opening of small cages containing harmless animals; the daubing of walls with paint. The others were grave, the letting-out of lethal animals such as Polar bears and tigers. The press immediately seized upon these events and shouted that a

Phantom was at work. The idea was nonsense, of course, but as soon as I was called in by Hardcastle my original impressions formed by the newspaper reports were reinforced."

Solar Pons paused and blew a cloud of aromatic blue smoke toward the ceiling as he gazed sternly downward at the deflated figure of Sir Clive.

"In all the trivial cases, where the person responsible could have simply opened catches or bolts, the doors of the cages had been smashed. Yet in the cases of the larger animals where there were heavy doors and stout padlocks, the intruder had not smashed them, but instead had used a key, which argued inside knowledge."

"It is interesting, Pons, but I do not quite see... " I began.

Solar Pons transfixed me with a look.

"It was elementary, my dear Parker. Two different people were the authors of the events. Hodgson, motivated by revenge, was determined to throw suspicion on his rival, young Hardcastle, for the affections of Miss Westover. That is understandable, if contemptible. But Hodgson, though unbalanced by jealousy, was conditioned by training and respect for his calling. He would not endanger human life in his scheme to discredit his rival. And though he committed damage it was extremely trivial. Sir Clive had access to all the keys or could have had them copied, so he avoided the noise which would have been made late at night by smashing the heavy locks. It was as simple as that. That was one of the striking differences and I at once concluded there were two strands to the affair. The mystery and the ensuing publicity were a godsend to Sir Clive. He had long been blackmailed by Jefferies, as is made clear by the correspondence I have read, and had been bled white. The so-called Phantom's activities provided him with an excellent opportunity, so a few weeks ago he began his own series of atrocities, which were of a far more serious kind; ranging from the freeing of dangerous spiders to the tigress and Polar bear. They had to be dangerous creatures to make the death of Jefferies more plausible."

Sir Clive passed a handkerchief across his streaming face with shaking fingers.

"You are right, Mr. Pons," he said. "I must have been mad but you cannot judge me unless you know the full circumstances."

"I am not presuming to judge you, Sir Clive," said Solar Pons, rubbing his chin. "That is not my function and I leave it to those better qualified."

"Jefferies has had thousands from me," said Sir Clive wearily. "We had been rivals for years. And the damnable thing is that he used much of the money to build new facilities at the Zoo and so gain fresh kudos for his own name." He turned burning eyes on my companion. "How on earth did you know, Mr. Pons?"

Solar Pons shook his head.

"It was mere suspicion at first, but it strengthened as my investigations continued. As I have said the pattern was so different in the two sets of incidents. I have already explained how I came to suspect Hodgson and Miss Westover confirmed the matter. But I very soon realised that the person who had been loosing the larger mammals had access to a large portion of the Zoo. Furthermore, no one suspicious had been seen either in or just outside the grounds. Therefore the miscreant had to be someone who could move about the Zoo, particularly at night, without attracting suspicion. A member of the staff or a high-ranking official. When I saw that your house adjoined the grounds and that a gate gave access to the Zoo premises my suspicions crystallised."

"So that was why you said something further might happen, Pons!" I exclaimed.

Solar Pons nodded.

"But even I did not realise what a tragic turn events would take. I had to make sure. Hodgson was nothing. I could have exposed him at any time. What I wanted to learn was why the more serious incidents were taking place. Well, we have found out." He looked at the smouldering remnants of the fire in the grate, his deep-set eyes seeming to gaze far beyond them. "The pattern was repeated in the near-tragic incident of the Polar bear. I retrieved from its claws a length of grey thread." He produced the small transparent paper envelope from his pocket as he spoke. "I immediately identified it as coming from a suit of good material. When I saw that Sir Clive wore a grey suit today and that a button was missing from the three on his right sleeve, I knew that he had had a narrow escape when releasing the beast from the enclosure. And I also knew that I had my man though I did not then know he was a potential murderer. The keepers wore coarse blue uniforms and the threads did not match."

He picked up the limp arm of the recumbent President and held up his sleeve for me to see. There was a button missing and I noticed immediately that the thread was a perfect match to that on the Director's coat. Sir Clive was breathing stertorously and he struggled into a more erect position.

"I submit that Jefferies called here tonight, probably for another payment or perhaps to hand over some letters," Pons went on. "You had already prepared the ground and you struck him on the neck with that heavy iron poker in the fireplace, when his back was turned. It was a foggy evening when you were unlikely to be seen and it was this which prompted you to make the appointment. When you had killed your tormentor you dragged him out through the French windows, with the study in darkness, of course, and down the path into the Zoo grounds. The public had long gone and there would be very few staff about on such a night. You counted on that."

"You are a devil, Mr. Pons," said Sir Clive softly, his eyes never leaving Pons' face.

"Hardly, Sir Clive. Merely a person devoted to justice. I could not fail to see the heel-marks of your victim in the grass of the lawn. Though no doubt they will be gone by morning if there is rain. And in any case who would be able to see them in the current foggy weather."

"But how would Sir Clive get the body to the gorilla-house, Pons?" I asked.

Solar Pons shrugged his lean shoulders.

"That was the easiest part, Parker. Probably one of the keepers' wheel-barrows. It would have taken only a moment to have tipped Jefferies in. I noticed two barrows in the gorilla-house. Apart from that the gorilla is a vegetarian. And Jefferies was an expert on them. Sir Clive used a key again on this occasion as he needed to be quick—and quiet. And then smashed the glass on his way out to attract attention to the murder, doing it from the wrong side in the stress of the moment."

"You are right, Mr. Pons," said Sir Clive, his eyes still open and staring.

"But you had noticed, as did I, that Jefferies had been bleeding slightly from the mouth," Pons continued. "You found, as I have already ascertained, that there were flecks of blood on the study floor. You wished to burn the documents on the desk there but there was no wood. And you also needed a cloth. You went out for both which gave me an opportunity to read some of the letters."

Sir Clive sat now with his head in his hands, his heavy breathing the only sign of life.

"There is just one flaw, Pons," I said. "Sir Clive's servants would know Jefferies had been here. They would have told the police tomorrow."

"Certainly, Parker. But I have no doubt Sir Clive would have mentioned it himself. But Mr. Jefferies would have left a good while before his body was found. Sir Clive would not know whether he had used the side-gate into the Zoo or not. And in any event I have no doubt that he would have let Jefferies out when none of the servants were about. And have made sure to have wished him good-night as loudly as possible."

"You think of everything, Pons."

"On the contrary, Parker, it is Sir Clive who has given this matter much thought. I am merely the humble instrument of justice."

"Justice, Mr. Pons? You call it justice?"

Sir Clive sat up and removed his hands from his face. He looked at us bitterly.

"Yes, Mr. Pons, I did all those things. You are correct in every respect. But if ever a man deserved to die it was Jefferies. A fouler creature never walked in shoe-leather. I am not sorry he is dead. I should have done it sooner. But I want you to believe that I would never have let Hodgson take the blame for my crime."

"I have no doubt of that, Sir Clive," said Pons steadily. "And if I know my man, Superintendent Heathfield will have discovered his innocence already."

Sir Clive stood up, his features working.

"Would you give me a quarter of an hour, Mr. Pons? I wish to take care of some things in the next room yonder."

Solar Pons nodded, his manner abstracted.

"Certainly, Sir Clive."

We waited as his footsteps died out across the parquet. My companion stared at me sombrely.

"It is a tragic business, Parker." He indicated the letters on the table. "A man's sexual aberrations are his own problem. In my view there is no crime so long as he does not corrupt the young. Sir Clive's peculiarities had brought him within the scope of the blackmailer, just as thousands have been in the past and many more will be in the future."

"Good heavens, Pons, I did not realise . . . "

Solar Pons smiled thinly. He went over to the desk and scooped up the letters. He placed them in the hearth, brought some logs over and stirred the embers into a blaze. Within a few minutes there was nothing but a handful of grey ashes in the fireplace.

"That will take care of an ugly scandal, Parker. The letters from Jefferies that I have retained will provide the police with enough motive, I think." He paused as there came the muffled crack of an explosion. I was already rushing toward the door when Solar Pons stopped me. "It is too late, Parker. I will not say that justice has been done, but the law will be satisfied. It is an imperfect world and we shall have to be content and let it rest there."

He stood in silence for a moment, putting the documents into his pocket, listening to the noise of hurrying footsteps in the house. Then he walked slowly toward the door of the room in which Sir Clive had just taken his life.

The Adventure of the
Frightened Governess

✐ 1

"WAKE UP, PARKER! It is six o'clock and we have
pressing matters before us."

I struggled into consciousness to find the night-
light on at the side of my bed and Solar Pons' aquiline features
smiling down at me.

"Confound it, Pons!" I said irritably. "Six o'clock! In the
morning?"

"It is certainly not evening, my dear fellow, or neither of us
would have been abed."

I sat up, still only half-awake.

"Something serious has happened, then?"

Solar Pons nodded, his face assuming a grave expression.

"A matter of life and death, Parker. And as you have been
such an assiduous chronicler of my little adventures over the
past years, I thought you would not care to be left out, despite
the inclement hour."

"You were perfectly correct, Pons," I said. "Just give me a few
minutes to throw on some things and I will join you in the
sitting-room."

189

Pons rubbed his thin hands briskly together with suppressed excitement.

"Excellent, Parker. I thought I knew my man. Mrs. Johnson is making some tea."

And with which encouraging announcement he quitted the room.

It was a bitterly cold morning in early February and I wasted no time in dressing, turning over in my mind what the untimely visitor to our quarters at 7B Praed Street could want at such a dead hour.

I had no doubt there was a visitor with a strange or tragic story to tell or Pons would not have disturbed me so untimely, and as I knotted my tie and smoothed my tousled hair with the aid of the mirror, I found my sleepy mind sliding off at all sorts of weird tangents.

But when I gained our comfortable sitting-room, where the makings of a good fire were already beginning to flicker and glow, I was not prepared for the sight of the tall, slim, fair-haired girl sitting in Pons' own armchair in front of the hearth. The only indication of anything serious afoot was the paleness of our visitor's handsome features. She made as though to rise at my entrance but my companion waved her back.

"This is my old friend and colleague, Dr. Lyndon Parker, Miss Helstone. I rely on him as on no other person and he is an invaluable helpmate."

There was such obvious sincerity in Pons' voice that I felt a flush rising to my cheeks and I stammered out some suitable greeting as the tall young woman gave me her cool hand.

"A bitterly cold morning, Miss Helstone."

"You may well be right, Dr. Parker, but I must confess my mind is so agitated that I have hardly noticed."

"Indeed?"

I looked at her closely. She did not seem ill but there was an underlying tension beneath her carefully controlled manner which told my trained eye there was something dreadfully wrong.

There was a measured tread upon the stair and the bright, well-scrubbed features of our landlady, Mrs. Johnson, appeared round the door. She was laden with a tray containing tea things and as I hastened to assist her I caught the fragrant aroma of hot, buttered toast.

"I took the liberty of preparing something for the young lady to sustain her on such a cold morning."

"Excellent, Mrs. Johnson," said Pons, rubbing his thin hands. "As usual, you are a model of thoughtfulness."

Our landlady said nothing but the faint flush on her cheeks showed that the deserved praise had not gone unnoticed. She hastened to pour out the tea and after handing a cup to Miss Helstone with a sympathetic smile, quietly withdrew.

"Will you not draw closer to the fire, Miss Helstone?"

"I am perfectly comfortable here, Mr. Pons."

"You have come from out of London, I see?"

"That is correct, Mr. Pons."

Pons nodded, replacing his cup in the saucer with a faint clink in the silence of the sitting-room.

"I see a good deal of mud on your boots which means you have been walking on an unmade road."

"It is a fair stretch to the station, Mr. Pons, and I was unable to get transport at that time of the morning."

"Quite so, Miss Helstone. You are not more than an hour out of town, I would surmise. Surrey, perhaps?"

Our client's surprise showed on her face as she took fastidious little sips at the hot tea.

"That is correct, Mr. Pons. Clitherington, a small village on the Redhill line."

Solar Pons inclined his head and favoured me with a faint smile as he bent forward in his armchair.

"That light, sandy soil is quite unmistakable, Parker. You no doubt noticed, as did I, a distinctive sample on the seams of the young lady's right boot."

I cleared my throat, caught unawares with a piece of toast halfway down.

"Now that you point it out, Pons, certainly."

"It is obviously something serious that brings you to us at this hour, Miss Helstone, and you have already told me it is a matter of life and death. You are equally obviously agitated beneath your calm manner. Please take your time. You are among friends."

The young woman drew in her breath with a long, shuddering sigh.

"That is good to know, Mr. Pons. It has indeed been quite unbearable this last day or two. And affairs at the house ... "

"You live there with your parents?" interrupted Pons.

The young woman paused and made an engaging little contraction of her mouth.

"I beg your pardon, Mr. Pons. I am telling the story very badly. I am engaged as a governess at The Priory, Clitherington, the home of Mr. Clinton Basden."

Solar Pons tented his thin fingers before him and gave our fair client his undivided attention.

"So far as I know, Miss Helstone, there is no train on the time-table which leaves a remote place like Clitherington at such an hour as four-thirty a.m."

Miss Helstone gave a faint smile, the first sign of returning normality she had evinced since I had entered the room.

"That is correct, Mr. Pons. I came up on the milk train. There are always two carriages used mainly by railway staff and I found an empty compartment."

"So that the matter is one of the utmost gravity. Pray continue."

"My full name is Helen Jane Helstone, Mr. Pons, and I come of a good family originally settled in the West Country. My parents were killed in a local uprising in India some years ago and after I had completed my schooling in England it became necessary to earn my living. I enjoy the company of children and so I became a governess with a view to entering a teacher-training college when I am a little older."

"What is your age now, Miss Helstone?"

"I am just turned twenty-one, Mr. Pons."

Solar Pons nodded and looked thoughtfully at the girl, who had now recovered the colour in her cheeks. She looked even more handsome than before and I found the contemplation of her most engaging but turned again to the tea and toast, aware of Pons' glance on me.

"I give this information, Mr. Pons, so that you shall know all of the salient circumstances."

"You are telling your story in an admirable manner, Miss Helstone."

"I had two positions, Mr. Pons, one in Cornwall and another in Cumberland, which I held for several years, but I decided to move nearer to London and when I saw Mr. Basden's advertisement in a daily newspaper, Surrey seemed ideal for my purposes and I hastened to answer his announcement."

"When was that, Miss Helstone?"

"A little over three months ago, Mr. Pons." Our visitor paused again and sipped at her tea; her face was thoughtful as though she were carefully contemplating her next words but my professional eye noted that her breathing was more regular and she was becoming calmer by the minute. "There was something extremely strange about my engagement as governess, Mr. Pons. I have often thought about it since."

"How was that, Miss Helstone?"

"For example, Mr. Pons, it was extraordinarily well-paid, though the duties are somewhat unusual."

Pons nodded, narrowing his deep-set eyes.

"Pray be most explicit, Miss Helstone."

"Well, Mr. Pons, I have no hesitation in telling you that the salary is some five hundred pounds a year, payable quarterly in advance."

Pons drew in his breath in surprise and I gazed at him open-mouthed.

"That is indeed princely for these times, Miss Helstone. I should imagine there would have been quite a few ladies in your position after the appointment."

"That is just it, Mr. Pons. There were literally queues. I met some people on the train who were answering the advertisement. Apparently it had been running in the daily newspapers for more than a week."

"That is highly significant, Parker," put in Pons enigmatically and he again resumed his rapt study of Miss Helstone's face.

Our client went on breathlessly, as though some reserve had been breached by the confidence my friend inspired in her.

"My heart sank, Mr. Pons, as you can well imagine but as the train stopped at Clitherington, my spirits rose again. You see, I had heard one of the girls say that though the announcement had been running for some time, the prospective employers were very fastidious and no one had yet been found to suit them."

"And as you already had experience of two similar appointments, you had high hopes?"

"Exactly, Mr. Pons. But my spirits were dashed when we arrived at the house. A large car had been sent to the station to meet applicants and we were taken to a vast, gloomy mansion, set in an estate whose main entrance was locked and guarded by heavily-built men."

"An odd circumstance, Miss Helstone," said Pons, glancing quizzically at me.

"You may well say so, Mr. Pons. But though the grounds, with their great clumps of rhododendron and pine plantations were gloomy and sombre indeed in that bleak December weather, the interior of the mansion was extremely luxurious and well appointed, evincing the most refined taste. It was evident that the prospective employer was a man of enormous wealth."

"And of fastidious nature if it took him so much time to select a governess for his children, Miss Helstone. How many were there, in fact?"

"Two, Mr. Pons. A boy and a girl, aged nine and twelve respectively. But my heart sank again, when we were shown into a sumptuously furnished drawing-room, to find between twenty and thirty young ladies already there."

"It sounds more like a theatrical producer's office, Pons," I could not resist observing.

Solar Pons gave me a faint smile and his eyes held a wry twinkle.

"Ah, there speaks the sybarite in you, Parker. The lover of night life, good wine and chorus girls."

"Heavens, Pons!" I stammered. "What will Miss Helstone think of me?"

"That you are a poor recipient of waggish remarks at your own expense, my dear fellow. But we digress."

Miss Helstone had smiled hesitantly at this little exchange, revealing two rows of dazzling white teeth.

"Well, there is a great deal of truth in Dr. Parker's remark, Mr. Pons," she said earnestly. "It did in truth look like a theatrical agency, though they are a good deal shabbier as a rule. But the most extraordinary thing was the proceedings. A hard-faced woman in black beckoned to the first girl as I sat down and she disappeared through the big double doors. In less than a minute she was back, with an angry shake of the head." Miss Helstone put down her cup and leaned forward in her chair, regarding my companion with steady grey eyes. "Mr. Pons, five of the applicants went in and out of that room in five minutes and it was obvious that none of them were suited by their angry expressions. But even more extraordinary—and I learned this afterwards—each and every one was given a new five pound note for her trouble, a car to the station and a free railway ticket to London."

Solar Pons clapped his hands together with a little cracking noise in the silence of the sitting-room.

"Excellent, Parker!" said he. "This gets more intriguing by the minute, Miss Helstone. There is more, of course."

"Much more, Mr. Pons. Of course, I got most intrigued as the minutes went by and the girls disappeared into the room. Those of us who were left moved up and fresh arrivals sat down behind us. Now and again there would be loud exclamations from behind the door and it was obvious as I got closer and closer to the double-doors guarded by the woman in black, that none of the girls had been found suitable by the mysterious advertiser. I did not, of course, at that stage, know the name of my employer, Mr. Pons, as it was not given in the advertisement."

"I see. It was a box number?"

"Exactly, Mr. Pons."

I got up at Pons' glance and refilled the teacups for all of us.

"But I was within three places of the door before a girl came out with whom I had travelled down from London. She was angry and had a heavy flush on her cheeks. She came across to me and had time for a few words before the woman, who was letting in a new applicant, came back. She said she was not asked for references or even any questions. A tall, dark woman was sitting at a desk and she looked at someone obviously sitting behind a heavy screen who was concealed from the applicant. He must have had some method of observing the candidate but in every case the answer had been no, for the woman merely nodded and said that the interview was closed. My informant said she was merely asked her name, address and if it were true that she was an orphan. It was obvious that even these questions were a mere formality."

"An orphan, Miss Helstone?"

Solar Pons had narrowed his eyes and on his face was the alert expression I had noted so often when moments of great enterprise were afoot.

"Why, yes, Mr. Pons. That was one of the stipulations of the advertisements. I have one here in my handbag. Another requirement was that applicants should be single or widows."

"Sounds most peculiar, Pons," I put in.

"Does it not, Parker?" Solar Pons glanced at the newspaper cutting Miss Helstone had passed to him and read it with increasing interest. "Just listen to this, Parker." He smoothed out the cutting on the table in front of him and read as follows:

"Young governess required for two small children in home of wealthy Surrey widower. Large mansion, congenial surroundings. Discretion essential, many advantages. Salary £500 per annum. No one over thirty need apply. Reply initially in writing and with two references. The position is for the benefit of orphaned young ladies only. Box 990."

Solar Pons frowned and looked at me quizzically.

"Extraordinary, is it not, Parker. I am obliged to you, Miss Helstone. Despite my enthusiasm for bizarre cuttings, this is something I missed. There are a number of unusual points, Parker."

"Indeed, Pons. The orphan stipulation is strange, to say the least."

"And tells us a great deal," said Solar Pons slyly. "Coupled with the lavish inducements it indicates a certain line of thought. What happened at your own interview, Miss Helstone?"

Our visitor put down her teacup and wiped her mouth fastidiously with a small lace handkerchief, waving away my proffered plate of toast.

"That was the most extraordinary thing of all, Mr. Pons. Within thirty minutes of my arrival at The Priory, thirty applicants had passed through those doors and then it was my turn. It was a large, though quite ordinary room, except for a circular window high up, which made it a dark, shadowy place. There was a desk underneath the window and a desk lamp alight on it, which threw the light forward on to a chair placed in front of the desk.

"A dark-haired, pleasant-looking woman with a central European accent asked me to sit down and then put to me some perfunctory questions. I naturally observed the large, heavy screen to the right of the desk and was then startled to see, in an angled mirror placed so as to favour my place on the chair, the reflections of a man's bearded face, with eyes of burning intensity."

2

There was another long pause which I employed in refilling my teacup. Miss Helstone leaned back in her chair and put out her hands to the fire, which was now blazing cheerfully.

"Some signal must have passed between the two because the woman at the desk gave a relieved smile and, as though making the decision herself, informed me that the position was mine. She called me over to another table in the corner and asked me to sign a document. I just had time to see that this asserted that I was an orphan, specified my age and verified my references, before I heard a door close softly somewhere. I was sure that the man behind the screen had quitted the room, Mr. Pons, and when we went back to the desk I could see that a chair placed behind the screen was empty."

Solar Pons rubbed his hands briskly.

"Admirable, Miss Helstone. This is distinctly promising. I may point out, by the way, that the document you signed has no legal standing whatsoever."

The girl smiled.

"I am glad to hear you say so, Mr. Pons. But that is the least of my worries. You may imagine the consternation and dismay among the young ladies in the ante-room when they heard the position was filled. I was astonished when Mrs. Dresden, the dark-haired woman, whom I then learned was the housekeeper, said I should start on my duties at once. But I prevailed upon her to let me return to my old employers to collect my luggage and to inform them of my new post, though even then they insisted on sending me by chauffeur-driven car in order to save time."

"You did not think this at all strange, Miss Helstone?"

"Strange indeed, Mr. Pons, but the salary was so princely that I did not hesitate, I was so excited."

"So you left The Priory without seeing your future charges?"

"That is correct, Mr. Pons. I was told the children were on holiday and would not be back until the following Monday.

"When I returned I was a little perturbed to see that the grounds were patrolled by similar men to those at the main gate and I realised then that I would not be free to get out and about as I had hoped and in the manner I had become used to in my other situations."

"You met this mysterious Mr. Basden?"

"Almost at once on my return, Mr. Pons. He was quite an ordinary little man, an Englishman obviously, and rather ill at ease, I thought, among the foreign-sounding employees among his retinue."

Solar Pons tented his fingers and stared at me sombrely.

"Does not that strike you as strange also, Parker?"

"Perhaps he had served in India, Pons?"

Solar Pons shook his head with a thin smile.

"I believe the young lady referred to Central Europeans, Parker."

"That is correct, Mr. Pons. There were other extraordinary requirements in my new duties also. For example, I was asked by the housekeeper to leave my own clothes in my room. She supplied me with a new wardrobe. They were very expensive clothes, Mr. Pons, but I had no objection, of course."

"Indeed," I put in.

"But then Mrs. Dresden asked me to put my hair up in a different style and gave me expensive jewellery to wear. I was a little apprehensive in case I lost any but was told not to worry as Mr. Basden was a very wealthy man. I was given the run of the magnificent house and was told I would be treated as a member of the family.

"I dined with Mr. Basden that evening and my impression of him being ill at ease in his own house was reinforced. He said little and after two days at The Priory I knew very little more about the post than when I arrived. I noticed one other odd thing, also. I could go almost anywhere I liked in the house, but there was a wing stretching off the main landing. I was forbidden to go there by Mrs. Dresden, as it was private.

"But I could not help seeing what went on, Mr. Pons. There were disturbances in the night once and I have seen what looked like nurses with trays of medicine. One morning also I surprised a tall, dark man on the stairs, with a little black bag. He looked grave and I was convinced he was a doctor."

Solar Pons leaned forward and his deep-set eyes stared steadily at the tall, fair girl.

"Just what do you think is in that wing, Miss Helstone?"

"Some sort of invalid, evidently, Mr. Pons. I did not enquire, naturally."

Solar Pons leaned back again in his chair and half-closed his eyes.

"And you have not seen the bearded man again since that first accidental glimpse at the interview?"

"Not at all, Mr. Pons. I had another shock when my two charges arrived. The children were attractive enough, but their voices were low and husky and I was told by Mrs. Dresden

201

they had colds. They seemed rather odd and sly and I was completely nonplussed when I found that neither spoke a word of English."

Solar Pons gave a low chuckle.

"Excellent, Miss Helstone."

The fair girl stared at my companion with very bright eyes.

"And what is more, Mr. Pons, I am convinced their father cannot speak their language either!"

"Better and better, Parker."

Miss Helstone stared at my companion in astonishment.

"I do not follow you, Mr. Pons."

"No matter, Miss Helstone. What was the next thing that happened in this extraordinary *ménage*?"

"Well, it was obvious, Mr. Pons, that I could not begin to conduct any lessons. When I pointed this out to Mrs. Dresden she said it was of no consequence as they had a tutor in their own tongue. I would be required for companionship; to take them on walks in the grounds; on motor-rides and to control their deportment."

"An unusual list of requirements and one which apparently commands a salary of five hundred pounds, Parker," said Pons, a dreamy expression on his face. "It gives one pause to think, does it not?"

"My words exactly, Pons."

"And when you hear that the walks were mostly conducted at night in the floodlit grounds of The Priory, you will begin to realise my perplexity, Mr. Pons."

My companion's eyes had narrowed to mere slits and he leaned forward, an intent expression on his face.

"The grounds were floodlit, Miss Helstone? And the walks were how many times a week?"

"About three times on average, Mr. Pons. Between ten o'clock and midnight."

"Unusual hours for small children, Parker."

"There is something wrong somewhere."

"For once you do not exaggerate, my dear fellow."

"The last three months have been strange ones for me, gentlemen," said our visitor, whose paleness had gone and whose natural vivacity had evidently returned, for her eyes were sparkling and her manner more animated.

"I took occasional meals with my employer; walked or drove with the children; read and played patience. I soon found that I was not allowed outside the gates alone, but I have learned that the art treasures in the house are so valuable that Mr. Basden is scared of burglars. I think myself he is afraid that his employees will be approached by criminal elements, for he insists that if one goes outside, then one does not go alone."

"Another curious circumstance which gives one much food for thought," observed Solar Pons.

"This was the odd routine of my life until a few weeks ago," Miss Helstone continued. "The people in the house were kind to me and I was well treated, but I felt circumscribed; almost imprisoned. The sealed wing was still barred to me and medicines and medical staff were in evidence from time to time, but nothing was explained and I did not think it circumspect to ask. But there was another peculiar circumstance; my employer does not smoke, or at least I have never seen him do so, yet I have on several occasions smelt strong cigar smoke in the children's room when I go to collect them for their walks. On one occasion there was a half-smoked cigar end on the windowsill and the little girl looked distinctly uneasy. I myself think that the bearded man had something to do with it."

Solar Pons looked searchingly at the girl.

"You think he may be the real father and not Mr. Basden?" Miss Helstone looked astonished.

"Those were my exact thoughts, Mr. Pons! You see, there is no genuine resemblance to Mr. Basden and the man with the beard had a foreign look."

"You may have stumbled on to something, Miss Helstone," Pons went on. "It is a most intriguing tangle that you have described. But you mentioned life and death?"

The girl swallowed once or twice and her eyes looked bleak.

"Twice in the past fortnight we have been accosted on our walks abroad, by strange, bearded men in a car. They spoke first to the children and then became very excited when I approached. I could swear they were all speaking the same language together. Yesterday a big black car tried to force ours off the road near Clitherington when we were out driving. Our chauffeur accelerated and drove back to the estate like a madman. We were all considerably shaken, I can tell you."

"Mr. Basden was informed of this?"

"At once. He looked white and ill and came down to apologise to me immediately."

Solar Pons pulled once or twice at the lobe of his right ear and looked at me quizzically.

"Which brings us to the early hours of this morning, Miss Helstone."

"I was walking in the grounds with the children last night, Mr. Pons. They sleep much during the day and their parent does not seem to mind their nocturnal habits. We had left the floodlit portion and followed the drive as it curved around. It was nearly midnight or a little after and we were about to turn back when there was a shot. It gave me such a shock, Mr. Pons!

The bullet glanced off a tree-trunk only a few feet from my head. I could hear guttural cries and I told the children to run."

"Highly commendable, Miss Helstone," I put in.

"Unfortunately, in their panic to escape they ran toward the voices," the girl went on. "Naturally, I had to go after them as they were my charges. We all got lost in the darkness, blundering about. I heard two more shots and then the same guttural voices I had heard from the men who had questioned the children on the road. I was so frightened, Mr. Pons, that I hid. I must have been in the woods for hours.

"I found myself in an unfamiliar part of the grounds; it was dark and cold and I did not know what to do. I was in an absolute panic. I had abandoned my charges, you see, and I did not know what might have happened to them. I could not face Mr. Basden. I found a small wicket-gate in the wall, which was unlocked; it may even have been used by the men to gain entrance to the grounds. Anyway, Mr. Pons, to bring a long and exceedingly rambling story to an end, I ran from The Priory and caught the milk train. I had read your name in the newspapers some months ago as being the country's greatest private detective so here I am to put my destiny in your hands."

3

Here our client paused and looked so appealingly at Pons that I could not forbear saying, "There, do not distress yourself further, little lady," while Pons himself looked at me disapprovingly.

"While deploring Parker's sentimental way of expressing it, I am in great sympathy with you, Miss Helstone. I have no hesitation in saying I will accept your case."

"Oh, thank you, Mr. Pons."

Helen Helstone rose from her chair and shook Pons' hand warmly. Pons looked at me interrogatively.

"Are you free, Parker?"

"Certainly, Pons. I have only to telephone my locum."

"Excellent."

He turned back to Miss Helstone.

"We must make arrangements to get you back to The Priory as soon as possible, Miss Helstone."

"Go back?"

Dismay and apprehension showed on the girl's face.

"It is the only way. We all want to know what went on there and I must confess I have not been so intrigued for a long while. And Parker and I will be with you."

"How are we going to manage that, Pons?" I said. "Considering that the estate is so well guarded."

"Tut, Parker," said Pons severely. "We have found Miss Helstone upon the road in the early hours of the morning when we were driving through the district, brought her home with us and are now returning her to her employer. The man Basden will have to see us. If there are such strange goings-on at his estate he will deem it imperative to discover just exactly what the outside world knows."

"Of course, Pons. I follow you."

Pons turned to our visitor.

"Do you feel up to it, Miss Helstone?"

"If you gentlemen will accompany me, Mr. Pons."

"That is settled, then."

The girl looked ruefully at her bedraggled coat and her muddied boots.

"If you will give me an hour or so, Mr. Pons, I must get to

the shops and purchase a few things."

"Certainly, Miss Helstone. If you will give me your parole?"

"I do not understand, Mr. Pons."

"If you will promise to come back within the hour."

Our visitor flushed and glanced from Pons to me.

"Of course, gentlemen. I am over my fright now and am as anxious to know what is happening at Clitherington as you."

"Very well, then." Pons looked at his watch. "It is a quarter past eight now. Shall we say ten o'clock at the latest."

"I will be here, Mr. Pons."

When I returned from showing our visitor to the front door Pons was pacing up and down in front of the fireplace, furiously shovelling blue smoke from his pipe over his shoulder.

"This beats everything, Pons," I said. "I have never come across such an extraordinary story."

"Does it not, Parker? What do you make of it? Let us just have your views."

"Well, Pons," I said cautiously. "I hardly know where to begin. There is something curious, surely, about the high salary being paid to this young lady for her purely nominal duties."

"You have hit the crux of the matter, Parker. Inadvertently, perhaps, but part of the central mystery, certainly."

"Ah, I am improving then, Pons," I went on. "But I confess that I cannot see far into this tangle. The children who speak a different language to their father; the nocturnal habits of such young people; the invalid in the sealed wing; the heavily guarded estate; the floodlit promenades. And who is the bearded man who sat behind the screen?"

Solar Pons took the pipe from between his strong teeth and looked at me with piercing eyes.

"Who indeed, Parker? You have retained the salient points

admirably and isolated the most important. You are at your most succinct, my dear fellow, and it is evident that my little lessons in the ratiocinative process have not been entirely lost."

"Let me have your views, Pons."

"It is foolish to theorise without sufficient data, Parker. But I see a few features which must resolve themselves with determined application. It is obvious why Miss Helstone was engaged but I would rather not speculate further at this stage."

"It is far from obvious to me, Pons," I said somewhat bitterly.

"Well, well, Parker, I am sure that if you employ your grey matter to good advantage, the solution will soon come to you."

And with that I had to be content until Pons returned from some mysterious errand of his own. I had just telephoned my locum when I heard his footstep upon the stair.

"I have hired a car, my dear fellow. If you will just step round to the garage in the next street and familiarise yourself with its controls, we will make our little expedition into the wilds of Surrey. Ah, here is Miss Helstone now."

Our client's step was light and she looked transformed as Mrs. Johnson showed her into the sitting-room.

"I am quite ready now, Mr. Pons."

Pons looked at her approvingly.

"Good, Miss Helstone. There are just a few preparations more. I have our plan of campaign mapped out. Parker, you will need your revolver."

"Revolver, Pons?"

"Certainly. I do not think the danger lies within the house. But the gentlemen who broke into the grounds appear to me to be an entirely different quantity altogether. Is there a tolerable inn in this village of Clitherington, Miss Helstone?"

"The Roebuck is very well spoken of, Mr. Pons."

"Excellent. We shall make that our headquarters, Parker."

I fetched my revolver and packed it in my valise. When I returned from the garage with the car, Pons and Miss Helstone were at the door of 7B in conversation with Mrs. Johnson, Pons well supplied with travelling rugs, for the day was a bitter one indeed. There was the usual tangle of traffic in town but I think I acquitted myself rather well, losing my way only once at a major junction, and we were soon well on the way to Surrey, the engine humming quietly while Pons and Miss Helstone, in the rear seats, conversed in low tones.

We arrived in the village of Clitherington about midday, smoke ascending in lazy spirals from the chimneys of the cluster of red-roofed houses which comprised the hamlet. As Miss Helstone had told us, the Roebuck was a comfortable, old-fashioned house with roaring fires and a friendly, well-trained staff. When we had deposited our baggage, Pons, Miss Helstone and I repaired to the main lounge for a warming drink after our journey while Pons put the finishing touches to our strategy.

As we sat at a side table he looked sharply at a tall, cadaverous man in a frock-coat of sombre colour, who was just quitting the room.

"Memory, Parker," he said sharply. "Quite going. Once upon a time I should have been able to recall that man in a flash. A doctor, certainly. And a Harley Street man if I mistake not. You did not see him?"

I shook my head.

"I was attending to the inner man, Pons. Is the matter of any importance?"

Pons shook his head. "Perhaps not, Parker, but the name is struggling to get out."

"Perhaps it will come later, Pons. In the meantime . . . "

"In the meantime we have much to do," he interrupted, draining his glass and getting to his feet. He smiled reassuringly at our companion. "And now, Miss Helstone, to penetrate your den of mystery."

꧁ **4**

A drive of about twenty minutes over rough, unmade roads, the traces of which Pons had already noted on our visitor's boots, brought us up against a high brick wall which ran parallel to the highway for several hundred yards.

"That is the wall of the estate, Mr. Pons," said our client in a low voice.

"Do not distress yourself, Miss Helstone," said Pons warmly. "I would not ask you to go inside again if I did not think it necessary. And, as I have already pointed out, you are in no danger from the occupants of The Priory unless I miss my guess. The shot came from the men who broke into the grounds; therefore the peril is from without."

Miss Helstone gave a relieved smile.

"Of course, Mr. Pons. You are right. But what could those men have wanted with me?"

"That is why we are here, Miss Helstone. Just pull over in front of those gates, Parker."

It was indeed a sombre sight as we drew near; the sky was lowering and dark and it was so cold that it seemed as though it might snow at any minute. The road ran arrow-straight past the high walls of the estate and two tall, gloomy iron gates with a lodge set next to them framed a drive that was lost among dark belts of trees.

I drew up at the entrance lodge and sounded the horn. Almost at once a roughly dressed, dark man appeared, a sullen look upon his face.

"Open the gates," I called above the noise of the engine. "Inform your master that Miss Helstone is here."

As I spoke our client showed herself at the rear passenger window and the big man's jaw dropped with surprise.

"One moment, sir. I must just inform the house," he said in a marked foreign accent.

He shouted something and a second man whom I had not seen set off at a run along the driveway and disappeared. I switched off the motor and we waited for ten minutes. All this time Pons had said nothing but I was aware of his comforting presence at my back. The sentry at the gate—for that was his obvious function—stood with arms folded behind the locked portals and stared impassively in front of him.

Then there was the sound of running footsteps on the drive and the second man reappeared, close behind him a tall, dark woman whom Miss Helstone immediately identified as Mrs. Dresden, the housekeeper. A short conversation followed, in a language with which I was not conversant, and then the first man unlocked the gates and drew them back. I drove through and Mrs. Dresden, who at once introduced herself, got into the rear of the car with Pons and our client.

"My poor child!" she said, obviously moved, and embraced the girl. "We thought something dreadful had happened to you."

"These gentlemen found me on the road and took me to their London home," Miss Helstone explained. "I was exhausted and incoherent, I am afraid. I explained the situation this morning and they kindly brought me back."

I was watching Mrs. Dresden closely in the rear mirror as I negotiated the winding driveway and I saw her look sharply at Pons.

"That was very good of them, my dear. Mr. Basden has been frantic with worry, I assure you. The children are quite safe."

"Thank God, Mrs. Dresden. I have been so concerned. What will Mr. Basden think? And what could those evil men have possibly wanted?"

The housekeeper faltered and I saw a look of indecision pass across her face.

"Do not trouble yourself further, Miss Helstone. Mr. Basden will explain. He is waiting for you. And he will certainly want to thank these gentlemen."

I drove on for some way and then the estate road widened out into a gravel concourse. I was prepared for an imposing building but the fantastic folly which rose before us in the darkling winter morning was a Gothic monstrosity on the grand scale, with turrets like a French *château* and crenellated walls grafted on. All surrounded by sweeping banks of gloomy rhododendrons, interspersed here and there with groups of mournful statuary, which seemed to weep in the moist air.

I stopped the car before a massive flight of steps, at the top of which another bulky, anonymous-looking man waited to receive us. I felt somewhat apprehensive but Pons looked immensely at home as he descended from the vehicle and looked approvingly about him with keen, incisive glances.

"You have not exaggerated, Miss Helstone. The Priory is indeed a remarkable piece of architecture."

Our client said nothing but took Pons' arm timidly as he mounted the steps after the hurrying figure of the housekeeper. She paused at the imposing front entrance to the house.

"Whom shall I say, sir?"

"My name is Bassington," said Pons in clear, pleasant tones. "And this is my friend, Mr. Tovey."

"A ridiculous name, Pons," I whispered as Mrs. Dresden disappeared through the portals and we followed at a more leisurely pace.

"Perhaps, Parker, but it was all I could think of at the moment. It is not unpleasing, surely? The name of a distinguished musician came into my mind."

"As you wish, Pons," I said resignedly. "I only hope I can remember it."

We were being ushered into a vast hall floored with black and white tiles now, and we waited while Mrs. Dresden and our client hurried up the marble staircase to the upper floors.

I looked round curiously, only half-aware of the bustle in the great house; it was evident that Miss Helstone's return had caused quite a stir and I could hear a man's voice raised in tones of relief. The mansion itself was magnificently appointed and all the strange circumstances of our client's story came back as I took in the details of our opulent surroundings.

We stood there for perhaps ten minutes, Pons silently observing the dark-coated men who scurried about the hall on furtive errands of their own, when a man came hurrying down the staircase. From his appearance and his timid air, I recognised the figure described so eloquently by Miss Helstone as Basden, the head of this strange household.

"Mr. Bassington?" he said in a trembling voice. "I am indeed indebted to you for the rescue of our little Miss Helstone. I have been distraught with worry. Mr. Tovey, is it? Do come into the drawing-room, gentlemen. Miss Helstone will join us once she has removed her hat and coat."

He led the way into a large, pine-panelled room in which an aromatic fire of logs burned in the marble Adam fireplace.

"Please be seated, gentlemen. May I offer you coffee or some stronger refreshment?"

"That is indeed good of you, Mr. Basden," said Pons blandly. "But speaking for myself I require nothing."

I smilingly declined also and studied Basden closely while his conversation with Pons proceeded. He did indeed look furtive and ill at ease, and constantly glanced about him as if we were being observed, though we were quite alone in the room.

"And how are the children?"

Basden looked startled and then collected himself.

"Oh, quite well, Mr. Bassington. They were merely frightened and ran back to the house. But I am not quite sure how you came across Miss Helstone..."

"We were on our way back to London in the early hours when we found the young lady bedraggled and half-conscious, lying by the side of the road. We got her into our car and as my companion is a doctor we thought it best to take her straight to my London house, where my wife made her comfortable overnight. In the morning, when she was sufficiently recovered, she told us her story and so we brought her immediately back."

Basden licked his lips.

"I see. As I have already indicated, that was extremely good of you both. If there is any way in which I could defray your expenses..."

Pons held up his hand with an imperious gesture.

"Say no more about it, Mr. Basden. But they sound a dangerous gang of ruffians about your estate. Ought we not to call in the police?"

The expression of alarm that passed across Basden's features was so marked it was impossible to mistake, though he at once attempted to erase it.

"We have had a good deal of trouble with poachers, Mr. Bassington," he said awkwardly. "My gamekeepers have dealt with the problem. We called the police, of course, but unfortunately the rogues got clean away without trace. The neighbourhood has been much plagued with the rascals."

"Oh well, that would appear to dispose of the matter," said Pons with a disarming smile. "I am glad it was no worse. And now, if we could just say goodbye to our young companion, we will be on our way."

"Certainly, Mr. Bassington. And a thousand thanks again for all your trouble."

We had just regained the hall when our client came hurrying down the stairs, the worry and strain of the past time still showing plainly on her face.

"Going so soon, gentlemen? I had hoped you would be staying to lunch."

"We have to get back to London immediately, Miss Helstone. But we leave you in safe hands, I'm sure."

Basden beamed in the background, one of the dark-coated men holding the hall-door ajar for us.

Pons bent his head over Miss Helstone's fingertips in a courteous gesture. I was close to him but even I had difficulty in making out the words he breathed to the girl.

"Have no fear, Miss Helstone. You are not in any danger. The doctor and I will be just outside the estate. Make sure you show yourself in the grounds tonight at about eight o'clock."

"Goodbye, gentlemen. And thank you."

There was relief on Miss Helstone's face as she and Basden said goodbye. The latter shook hands with us briefly and the two of them stood on the front steps watching us as we drove away. I had noticed previously that there were other cars in front of the house and Pons seemed to show great interest in a gleaming Rolls-Royce Silver Ghost which was parked near the steps. As soon as we had been passed through the entrance gates by the guards and were rolling back toward Clitherington, Pons became less reticent.

"Well done, Parker. You played your part well. What did you think of The Priory?"

"Miss Helstone had not done it justice, Pons. But I judge it to be an elaborate façade."

"Excellent, Parker! You improve all the time. If Basden is master there I will devour my hat in the traditional manner. Just pull into the verge here like a good fellow, will you. I have a mind to engage in conversation with the owner of that Rolls-Royce when he comes out."

"But how do you know he is coming this way, Pons?" I protested.

Solar Pons chuckled, his face wreathed in aromatic blue smoke as he puffed at his pipe.

"Because, unless I am very much mistaken, the gentleman concerned is staying at the very same hostelry as ourselves. I assume that he would have remained at The Priory in order to let us get well clear."

"What on earth are you talking about, Pons?"

Pons vouchsafed no answer so I pulled the car up in a small lay-by at the end of the estate wall, where the road curved a little. We had not been sitting there more than ten minutes when Pons, who had been studying the road keenly in the rear mirror, which he had adjusted to suit himself, gave a brief exclamation.

"Ah, here is our man now. Just start the engine and slew the vehicle round to block the road, will you?"

I was startled but did as he bid and a few seconds later the big grey car glided up behind us and came to a halt with an imperious blaring of the horn. An irate figure at the wheel descended and I recognised the tall man in the frock coat whom Pons had pointed out in the bar of The Roebuck.

Pons bounded out of the passenger seat with great alacrity and beamed at the furious figure.

"Good morning, Sir Clifford. Sir Clifford Ayres, is it not? How goes your patient's health?"

The tall, cadaverous man's jaw dropped and he looked at Pons sharply, tiny spots of red etched on his white cheeks.

"How dare you block the road, sir? So far as I am concerned I do not know you. And I certainly do not discuss the private affairs of my patients with strangers."

"Come, Sir Clifford, you are remarkably obtuse for a Harley Street man. If you do not remember me, you must recall my distinguished colleague, Dr. Parker?"

Sir Clifford made a little gobbling noise like a turkey cock and stepped forward with white features, as though he would have struck Pons.

"By God, sir, if this is a joke I do not like it. My presence here was confidential. If you are press you will regret printing anything about me. I'll have you horsewhipped and thrown into prison. Clear the road or I will drive to the police immediately."

Pons chuckled and motioned to me to remove the car.

"Well, well, it does not suit your purpose to remember the Princes Gate reception last month, Sir Clifford. No matter. We shall meet again. Good day, sir."

And he politely tipped his hat to the apoplectic figure of

Ayres at the wheel and watched him drive on in silence. He was laughing openly as he rejoined me.

"Sir Clifford is noted for his fiery temper and bad manners and he is running true to form today. Either he genuinely did not recognise me or it obviously suits his purpose to plead ignorance. But it merely strengthens my suspicions about his patient."

"What is all this about, Pons?" I said as we drove on. "I must confess the matter becomes more confusing by the minute."

"All in good time, my dear fellow. I must contact Brother Bancroft when we get back to the inn and then I must purchase a daily paper. We shall have a busy evening if I am not mistaken."

And with these cryptic utterances I had to be content for the time being. We lunched well at The Roebuck and though Pons was obviously on the lookout for Sir Clifford, the tall doctor did not put in an appearance. We were eating our dessert before Pons again broke silence.

"Come, Parker, I need your help. You are obviously more *au fait* than I with Sir Clifford. Just what is his forté?"

"In truth I have never met the man, Pons," I said. "Though you seemed to think he should know me. I do not move in such exalted circles. As a humble G.P...."

"Tut, Parker, you are being too modest. My remark was merely meant to inform him that you were a fellow physician. We were introduced at the reception I spoke of but there were many people there; we were face to face for only a few seconds; and I relied on the traditional obtuseness of the medical profession and felt confident that he would not recall me."

"Come, Pons," I protested. "That is a definite slur."

Solar Pons chuckled with satisfaction.

"You are too easily ruffled, my dear fellow. You must practice indifference in such matters. But you have not answered my question."

"Sir Clifford? I know of his work, of course. He is one of the country's foremost specialists in heart disease and strokes."

"Indeed. I find that singularly interesting. This may not be so difficult as I had thought. If you will forgive me, I must telephone Bancroft. I will rejoin you for coffee in the lounge."

5

"Now, Parker, let us just put a few things together. In addition to the other small points we have already discussed, we have an eminent Harley Street specialist staying in this small place and in attendance on someone within The Priory. Does not that suggest a fruitful line of enquiry?"

Solar Pons sat back in a comfortable leather chair in the coffee-room at The Roebuck and regarded me through a cloud of blue pipe-smoke. It was early evening and the place was quiet, only the occasional rumble of a cart or the higher register of a motor-vehicle penetrating the thick curtains.

"Certainly, Pons. The invalid in the sealed wing suffers from heart trouble."

"Elementary, Parker. But why?"

Pons' brows were knotted with thought and his piercing eyes were fixed upon a corner of the ceiling as he pulled reflectively at the lobe of his right ear.

"I do not follow the question, Pons."

"It is no matter, Parker. Things are becoming clearer and I should be able to arrive at some definite conclusion before the evening is out."

"You surprise me, Pons."

Solar Pons looked at me languidly, little sparks of humour dancing in his eyes.

"I have often heard you say so, Parker. I have spoken to Brother Bancroft and he has given me some interesting information on affairs in Eastern Europe."

"I should have thought this was hardly the time for it, Pons."

"Would you not? However, it is no matter. My thoughts were directed to the subject by the events of the last day's newspapers. Apparently things in Dresdania are not going too well. Her Highness is out of the country and there is a concerted effort to unseat the government in her absence. Bancroft is most concerned."

"I must confess I am completely bewildered by your line of thought, Pons."

"Perhaps this will clarify matters."

Pons handed me a bundle of newspapers, among them *The Times* and *The Daily Telegraph*. I perused them with mounting puzzlement. In each case Pons had heavily ringed or marked certain items in ink. I caught the large heading of the *Daily Mail*: PRINCE MIRKO APPEALS FOR CALM. Apparently things in the state Pons had mentioned were in serious disarray.

"I must admit that The Balkans has increasingly occupied the world's thoughts, Pons," I observed. "Matters are constantly in ferment there and it is certain that our own Foreign Office has a definite interest in maintaining peace in that area of the world. But I know little about such affairs..."

Solar Pons chuckled, holding his head on one side as he looked at me.

"Do you not see the connection, Parker? Oh, well, there is

really no reason why you should. All will be made clear to you in due course. Now, you have your revolver handy, I trust?"

"It is in my valise in my room, Pons."

"Good. Just run along and fetch it, there's a good fellow. We may well have need of it before the night is out." He paused and stared at me sombrely. "Pray heaven we are in time, Parker. Either she is already dead or so ill that she cannot sign documents."

"Good Lord, Pons!" I cried. "If anything has happened to Miss Helstone through our neglect..."

To my astonishment Pons burst out laughing.

"Do not distress yourself, my dear fellow. I was not referring to Miss Helstone at all. You are on entirely the wrong tack."

He glanced at his watch.

"It is only just turned six o'clock. We have plenty of time. It is a fine night and we will walk, I think. As long as we are at the estate by eight we shall have ample room for manoeuvre."

It was a long and lonely walk, on a clear, moonlit night, though bitterly cold. As Pons and I, both heavily muffled, walked along the grass verge at the side of the road, with the wind whistling through the leafless branches of the trees which came down in thick belts of woodland close to the highway, I could not help reflecting on the anguish and terror which must have animated Miss Helstone when she ran along this same thorough-fare to catch the early morning train to bring her to Pons.

It wanted but a few minutes to eight when we arrived at the high wall of the estate belonging to The Priory. Pons' eyes were bright in the moonlight and his entire form seemed to radiate energy and determination.

"Now, Parker," he whispered, looking about him keenly.

"We will just cast about for the side-gate Miss Helstone mentioned. I have a feeling that it may be in use again this evening."

"I do not see how we are to get in, Pons. Basden's people may be watching the entrance there."

"We shall have to risk that, Parker. And I daresay I can get over the wall at a pinch, with the aid of your sturdy shoulders. But come what may, we must get inside The Priory tonight."

I followed Pons as he stepped off the road and we skirted the wall for something like a quarter of a mile, beneath the dark boughs of overhanging trees.

"We must go carefully now," Pons breathed. "It cannot be far. I questioned Miss Helstone carefully about this gate and it should be somewhere here, according to her description."

As he spoke the moonlight shimmered on a gap in the wall; a few strides more brought us to the gate in question. I looked at Pons swiftly but he had already noted what I had seen. The portal was slightly ajar. I had my revolver out and we crept forward quietly. Pons bent to examine the chain and padlock.

"Our friends are already in the grounds," he whispered. "Cut through with a hacksaw. They must have made some noise. It is my opinion, Parker, that Basden's employers mean to bring the game to them. Which merely substantiates my conclusions."

"I wish I knew what on earth you were talking about, Pons," I murmured irritably.

Solar Pons smiled thinly.

"Just keep your revolver handy, friend Parker, and follow me."

He disappeared quietly through the small gate which pierced the massive wall and I followed him quickly, finding myself in almost total darkness, the shrubbery grew so thickly and so close to the boundary the other side.

But as we went farther in, treading carefully and taking care to see we made as little noise as possible, the trees fell away and soon we found ourselves near the estate road along which we had driven earlier in the day. There was a strange light in the sky ahead and as we rounded a bend, skirting the drive and keeping well into the thick undergrowth, the façade of The Priory suddenly sprang sharply into view, clear-etched in the floodlights.

"The little charade seems to be successful," said Pons drily. "Now, just keep a sharp look-out, Parker. You are an excellent shot and I should not like the men who have preceded us through that wicket-gate to come upon us unawares."

I knelt by his side and looked around somewhat uneasily. We were well concealed here but through the fringe of leafless branches we had a good view of the house with its lawns and statuary. Even as we settled, the slim figure of Miss Helstone and two small children were descending the steps.

"Ah, they are early this evening, Parker," said Pons with satisfaction. "It seems that things are expected to happen. If I were you I should just throw off the safety-catch of your revolver, there's a good fellow."

I obeyed Pons' injunction, secretly puzzled at his remarks. Our client, after pausing initially at the foot of the steps, was now coming toward us across the grass, while the children shouted and ran in circles about her. Their shadows, caught by the glare of the floodlighting, cast long replicas before them across the lawn.

I was shifting my position when I was almost thrown off-balance by my companion seizing my arm.

"There, Parker, there! We are just in time to avert tragedy."

I followed his pointing finger and saw the bushes move at the other side of the drive. Then I became fully aware of what his keen eyes had already discerned. A thin, dark man with a pointed beard, down on one knee, crouched over a black rectangle which glinted as he moved. Pons was up like a flash and running back down the verge, away from the figure in the bushes. I was only a yard away as we crossed the roadway behind him.

"Your bird, I think, Parker," Pons called as the bearded man turned. The flare of light was followed by the slap of the shot and I heard the bullet whistle somewhere through the bare branches. I was cool now and sighted the revolver carefully as I squeezed the trigger. The rifle went off in the air as the man dropped.

The night was suddenly full of cries and noise; heavy bodies blundered about the bushes. I saw Miss Helstone frozen in mid-stride, the two children running from her. I dropped to the gravel as more shots sounded. Then Pons was beside me and urging me up.

"We must get to the young lady, Parker."

A group of dark figures had debouched from the terrace and were running down the grass; I heard a whistle shrill. Miss Helstone's face was white as we drew near. But the children were before her. The little girl's face was twisted. I saw the knife glint and was astonished to see Pons fell her with a deft blow from the flat of his hand. The knife fell on the grass and I levelled my revolver at the little boy who was barking orders in a strange, guttural language. He sullenly let the barrel of the pistol in his hand sag toward the ground.

"What does all this mean, Mr. Pons?"

Helen Helstone's face was white, her eyes wide in astonishment.

"That the charade is over, Miss Helstone. You are quite safe now and have nothing to fear."

"I do not understand, Mr. Pons. The children..."

Solar Pons smilingly shook his head and went to help the little girl up.

She was quite unhurt and kicked him on the shin for his pains.

"Not children, but midgets, Miss Helstone," said Pons gravely. "Evidently to guard your safety. I will give the Prince that much, at any rate."

"What is all this, Pons?" I began when a sullen ring of dark figures closed in on us. Others appeared behind, bringing with them three roughly-dressed men with beards; one was wounded and had a blood-stained handkerchief clapped to his wrist. A tall man detached himself from the group which had come from the terrace. He had a commanding air and his eyes glittered.

"Drop that revolver!" he ordered me. "You will find it is a good deal easier to get in than to get out."

Solar Pons smiled pleasantly.

"On the contrary. I beg you not to be foolish. Just inform Prince Mirko that we are here and that we have averted a tragedy."

The big man's face was puzzled. His English was almost perfect but his sudden agitation made him stumble over the words as he replied.

"Who are you?"

"My name is Solar Pons. Just give the Prince my card, will you, and tell him that the British Foreign Office knows we are here and will hold him responsible for our safety and that of Miss Helstone."

The tall man stood in silence for a moment, studying the card Pons had given him, while the floodlights beat down their golden light on the melodramatic tableau on the broad lawn, turning the faces of ourselves and the guards into ashen masks.

"Very well, Mr. Pons," the tall man said at last, lowering his pistol. "We will all go into the house."

6

"I think you owe me an explanation, Mr. Pons."

The tall man with the quavering voice took a step forward and regarded Solar Pons with indignation. The big room with the opulent appointments seemed full of people; apart from ourselves there were a number of armed guards and the sullen captives. Only Solar Pons seemed supremely at ease as he stood, an elegant, spare figure, and regarded our host thoughtfully.

"On the contrary, Mr. Basden, it is you who must explain yourself."

"I do not know what you mean."

"Oh, come, Mr. Basden, if that is really your name. Shots, a murderous attack, threats, armed guards. To say nothing of the danger to Miss Helstone, a British subject. His Britannic Majesty's Government would not take kindly to a Balkan enclave within a friendly sovereign state."

Basden stepped back, his face turning white; he looked as if he were about to choke.

"Pray do not discompose yourself," said Solar Pons. "My guess is that you are an excellent actor, hired for the occasion, but a little out of your depth. Now, if you will kindly ask

Prince Mirko to step out from behind that screen in the corner, we will proceed to hard facts." Pons turned a mocking gaze toward the screen in question; now that he had directed my attention to it I could see a thin plume of blue smoke rising from behind it. "How is Her Royal Highness' health this evening, Prince?"

There was an angry commotion and the screen was flung violently to the ground. A huge man with a thick beard stood before us, his eyes burning with rage.

"Why, that is the gentleman I glimpsed at my interview, Mr. Pons!" said Miss Helstone in surprise.

"Allow me to present His Highness, Prince Mirko of Dresdania," said Pons. "Your real employer and the instigator of this elaborate farce."

Mirko had recovered himself.

"Hardly a farce, Mr. Pons," said Mirko levelly, regarding Pons with a steady gaze from wide brown eyes. "You have unfortunately penetrated to the heart of Dresdania's secrets and you may find the price a high one to pay."

"I think not," said Solar Pons coolly. "My brother Bancroft holds an eminent position in the Foreign Office. If anything happens to us, troops will be here in short order." He broke off and glanced at his watch. "In fact, you have an hour to give me a satisfactory explanation of this affair."

There was an air of grudging admiration about Prince Mirko as he stared evenly at Pons.

"You do me a grave disservice, Mr. Pons," he said quietly. "I wish you no harm and I have certainly done my best to protect Miss Helstone."

"After first putting her life at peril."

Mirko shrugged his massive shoulders.

"Politics, Mr. Pons. Dresdania must come first with us. I implied no physical threat by my remark about paying a high price. Merely that the British Government will find the Balkans aflame if my efforts fail. Let us lay our cards on the table, shall we?"

"By all means," said Solar Pons equably. "Will you start or shall I?"

The Prince smiled grimly and led the way across to the far door. He said something in a foreign tongue to the big man who led the guards and they trooped from the room with their prisoners.

"We will be more comfortable in the library, Mr. Pons. Will not you, the lady and the doctor sit down? Ah, I think you already know Sir Clifford Ayres."

The tall, sour figure of the Harley Street man uncoiled itself from an armchair and came down the room toward us. He held out his hand stiffly, embarrassment clear on his face.

"I must apologise for my earlier rudeness, Mr. Pons; Dr. Parker. I could not breach the code of professional conduct, as you well know. I did remember you from the reception, Mr. Pons."

"Good of you to acknowledge it, Sir Clifford," said Pons smoothly, as we seated ourselves. "This is an unfortunate affair but events appear to have taken a turn for the better. How is the man Dr. Parker shot?"

"Dead, Mr. Pons," said the Prince. He waved me down as I started to get up from my chair. "You need not distress yourself, Dr. Parker. Krenko was one of the most murderous scoundrels who ever walked in shoe-leather. You have done Dresdania a great service tonight, doctor, for which she cannot thank you enough."

I cleared my throat.

"Thank goodness for that, anyway, Pons. I should not like the thing to lie heavily on my conscience. And then there is the little matter of the police..."

Pons smiled.

"That is the least of our problems, Parker. You must just content yourself with knowing that you have saved Miss Helstone."

"At your instigation, Pons. I am completely baffled."

"And yet the matter was a fairly simple one, Parker, merely requiring the key. I am sure Prince Mirko will correct me if I am wrong, but it was obvious from the moment Miss Helstone consulted us that she was not required for duties as a governess; neither was she being paid five hundred pounds a year for her undoubted skills in that area."

"But for what Pons?"

"For a masquerade, my dear fellow. For her remarkable resemblance to the Princess Sonia, the ruler of Dresdania. Everything pointed to it. And as soon as I saw the Princess' picture in the newspapers, the whole thing became clear. The interview with Mr. Basden—he is an actor in your employ, is he not?—the man behind the screen who was making the selection; and the quite extraordinary way in which Miss Helstone alone from all the hundreds interviewed suddenly fitted the bill. She could not even speak the same language as her charges.

"But it was crystal-clear that the sole object of her employment was her unwitting impersonation of an absent person, even to changing her hair-style; wearing unaccustomed jewellery and expensive clothing; and to being seen late at night beneath the floodlighting outside this house. The whole thing smacked of the stage, Parker."

Prince Mirko gave a wry smile and studied the tip of his cigar.

"I can now see why Mr. Pons is spoken of as England's greatest consulting detective," he observed to Sir Clifford.

Helen Helstone's eyes were wide as she turned toward Pons.

"Of course, Mr. Pons. It is so simple when you put it like that. I had not thought of it."

"Exactly, Miss Helstone. And there was no reason why you should. But it is at least to the Prince's credit that while tethering you as a decoy he at least provided you with adequate bodyguards."

"It was a regrettable necessity," said Prince Mirko. "Dictated by the inexorable requirements of the State."

"And a most original method," said Pons reflectively. "They looked exactly like children. And they are potentially deadly."

He rubbed his shin with a slight grimace. Prince Mirko's smile broadened.

"They are the Zhdanov Twins, circus and music-hall performers. Boy and girl. They specialise in the impersonation of children and both are expert at Ju-Jitsu, knife and pistol. You were lucky they did not shoot you first and ask questions afterwards. We have several times used them in our secret service operations."

"But how could you know this, Pons?" I cried.

"It was a fairly rapid process to the trained mind, Parker. I soon came to the conclusion they were midgets. The harshness of voice; the fact that they stayed out so late at night, which no real children would do; their peculiar actions when the attempt was made on Miss Helstone's life." His smile widened. "You remember they ran toward the source of danger when Miss Helstone's life was attempted. That was significant. To say nothing of the male twin's cigar-smoking in their rooms. The lady suspected that you were the parent in the case, Prince."

The bearded man bowed ironically to our client.

"That was most careless and I will see that the guilty party is reprimanded."

"Your prisoners, Prince," put in Solar Pons sharply, as though the idea had only just occurred to him. "No Dresdanian summary justice on British soil."

"It shall be as you say, Mr. Pons," said Prince Mirko. "In any case Dr. Parker has despatched the principal viper. And with the imprisonment of the others, the threat to Dresdania's internal politics is entirely removed."

"If you would be kind enough to elucidate, Pons!" I said hotly.

"My dear fellow. Certainly. If you had taken the trouble to read the newspapers properly this morning, they would have told you most of the story about Dresdania's internal troubles. It is Princess Sonia, is it not?"

Mirko nodded gravely.

"Her Royal Highness was in England incognito, on a short holiday. She is only thirty-eight, as you know. To our alarm and astonishment she had not been here more than three days when she was laid low by a crippling stroke. That was some four months ago. When she was well enough to be moved from a small, private nursing home near Epsom, we brought her here to this mansion, which belongs to the Dresdanian Embassy. Our own personnel surrounded her and we had the world's finest medical attention and nursing staff."

Here Sir Clifford bowed gratefully in acknowledgement of his services.

Solar Pons turned his lean, alert face toward the Prince.

"And how is Her Royal Highness at this moment?"

"Much improved, I am glad to say. It was a freak condition, I understand, and rare in one so young. I am assured by Sir Clifford that she will make a complete recovery. She will be well enough to sign State documents within the next few days."

"I am still not quite sure that I follow, Pons," I said.

"I see that you do not understand Balkan politics, doctor," said the Prince. He held up his hand. "And there is really no reason why you should. But Dresdania's internal stability is a vital element in the uneasy peace in that part of the world. Dissident elements have long been pledged to opposing the Throne and tearing it down. Vilest of them was Krenko; bombings, murder, political assassination and torture were only a few of the weapons he employed. As you know, the Princess is a widow and she has ruled as Regent, with me to guide her, on behalf of her son. He is now fourteen and of an age when he may soon be able to assume his responsibilities. Princess Sonia is anxious that he should do so, as the last decade has been a fearful strain. Indeed, it was probably this which precipitated the stroke. Her medical advisers prescribed complete rest and she came to England.

"But there was an attempted coup within a week of her arrival and unfortunately she was already ill. It was imperative for the country and for the sake of the young Crown Prince, who knows nothing of his mother's condition, that all should appear to be well."

"Hence the masquerade!" I put in. I stared at Pons in admiration. "And you saw all this at a glance?"

"Hardly, Parker. But it was not too difficult to arrive at the truth, once all the threads were in my hand."

Prince Mirko cast a regretful look at Miss Helstone.

"I must confess that I did not really think I would have much success with my ruse but I inserted the advertisement which Miss Helstone answered. I was in despair when I saw her at the interview but then realised what an astonishing likeness she had to the Princess."

Here he indicated a photograph in a heavy gilt frame which stood on a piano in one corner of the library.

"I determined to take a chance. It was a desperate act but the only card I had left to play. It was imperative that the Princess should be seen behaving normally. Hence the deception; the floodlighting and the nightly promenades. We had heard that Krenko and a band of desperadoes had arrived in England. He would either make an attempt on the Princess' life, in which case we would be ready and try to eliminate him; or, he would merely report back to his political masters that the Princess was well and carrying out her normal duties. Either would have suited us, because there is no fear of a coup while the Princess is alive—she is so popular among the common people. All we wanted was to stabilise things until the Princess should be well enough to sign the Instrument of Succession on behalf of her son. But Krenko evaded our vigilance and made an attempt on her life; we knew he would try again."

"For which purpose you put on a visible show of guarding the estate, while deliberately leaving the side-gate vulnerable," said my companion. "And you required an orphan in case of any tragic developments."

"Exactly, Mr. Pons. We had hoped that the presence of so distinguished a heart-specialist would pass unnoticed in the district—Sir Clifford insisted on staying at the inn where he could obtain his peculiarly English comforts—but we had not reckoned on your deductive genius."

"You are too kind, Prince Mirko." Pons consulted his watch. "I shall need to telephone Brother Bancroft, unless we wish the military to descend upon us."

Mirko nodded thoughtfully, the smoke from his cigar going up in heavy spirals to the library ceiling.

"It would be helpful if you would ask him for a responsible officer from Scotland Yard to attend to this affair, in conjunction with your Home Office and our Foreign Office, Mr. Pons."

"Superintendent Stanley Heathfield is your man, Prince," said Solar Pons, with a conspiratorial nod which took in myself and Miss Helstone. "If you will just excuse me." He paused by the door.

"It occurs to me, Prince Mirko, that Miss Helstone has been in considerable danger while under your roof. Now that her duties are prematurely ended, do you not think that some compensation is in order?"

"I had not overlooked that, Mr. Pons," said Mirko gravely. "My Government's cheque for twenty thousand English pounds will be paid into any bank of her choice."

"Twenty thousand pounds!"

Helen Helstone's face was incredulous as she gazed from me to Pons.

"The labourer is worthy of his hire, my dear young lady," Solar Pons murmured.

"And it is cheap for the security of the state," Prince Mirko added.

"I hardly know what to say, Mr. Pons,"

"Take the money, Miss Helstone. I assume that Mr. Basden has been well looked after?"

"You may rely upon it, Mr. Pons," said Mirko gravely. "Though an admirable actor, he is hardly ideal when called upon to play a part in which reality may intrude at any moment. His behaviour under stress has made him an unstable tool at times. And though we coached him carefully in the language, he forgot even those few phrases when under pressure."

Solar Pons returned from telephoning within a few minutes, rubbing his thin hands together.

"Excellent! Superintendent Heathfield is running down with a party of selected officers just as soon as train and motor-car can bring him. In the meantime I think our work here is ended, Parker. No doubt you will wish to come with us, Miss Helstone?"

"If you will just give me a few minutes to pack, Mr. Pons."

"Certainly. And I must emphasise that you must exercise the utmost discretion as to what you have heard in this room tonight."

"You have my word, Mr. Pons."

Mirko looked on with admiration.

"Mr. Pons, you should have been a diplomat."

"I leave all that to my brother, Prince Mirko," said my companion carelessly. "But I think that under the circumstances you would have done better to have taken our Foreign Office into your confidence."

"Perhaps, Mr. Pons," said Prince Mirko, studiously examining the glowing red tip of his cigar.

Sir Clifford Ayres rose to his feet and stiffly shook hands.

"A rapid convalescence and a complete recovery to your patient, doctor. And my congratulations."

"Thank you. Good night, Mr. Pons. Good night, doctor."

"Good night, Sir Clifford."

We waited in the hall as Miss Helen Helstone descended the

stairs, her face still bearing traces of the excitement of the night and of her unexpected good fortune. Prince Mirko took the paper bearing her address and studied it beneath the chandelier in the hallway, his bearded face enigmatic.

"Dresdania is grateful, young lady."

He brushed her hand with his lips and bowed us out. The Princess' car was waiting outside and conveyed us back to the high road.

"A remarkable achievement, Pons," I said, as soon as we were driving back in the direction of Clitherington.

"A case not without its points of interest, my dear fellow," he said with tones of approbation. He smiled across at our fair client. "They do things a great deal differently in the Balkans, Parker, but by his own lights Mirko has not done badly by Miss Helstone. By the time she marries—and providing she has handled her funds wisely—she will be a well-propertied woman."

And he lit his pipe with considerable satisfaction.

SOLAR PONS

7B, PRAED STREET
PADDINGTON, LONDON, W. 2   AMBASSADOR 10000